STUCK IN TIME

STUCK IN TIME

DAVE JOHNSON

Cover art by Jessica Bell
Illustrations by Elizabeth Newsham

ISBN: 978-1-7391326-0-6

For grandchildren everywhere, especially for my own:
Jake, Billy, Charlie, Amelie & Bertie.

All books are stand-alone stories

CHAPTER ONE

Lucy, Robert and James Baxter were all packed up and ready to leave school for the Easter holidays. Normally they would spend the Easter break at their boarding school, Greystones, and then visit their grandparents in Scotland during the summer holiday. It had been three years since their parents, celebrated historians and explorers, had disappeared on an expedition in South America. Now the children had settled into their new life; the routines and traditions of the school gave them a reassuring sense of security, but this holiday they were ready for a change. This time it was going to be different; they were going to stay with Uncle Archie. They had met him several times over the years but had never been to visit. Uncle Archie used to work for the government doing something very secret. They knew he ran a small private museum in Cambridge and had an apartment in the same building, and they knew that he was late!

Lucy looked at her watch for the tenth time in as many minutes.

'I can't stand it when people are late. Our Easter holiday should have started twenty minutes ago, and here we are… still here!'

She looked over at her two older brothers. No one would guess that they were twins. Robert was tall and sporty, with dark curly hair, whereas James was smaller, with a shock of unruly red hair. Normally, James was energetic, mischievous and noisy and always getting into trouble at school for playing tricks during lessons. However, today James was not his usual self.

'I feel peculiar,' he moaned as he curled himself up on the window seat in the school's reception area.

'You do look a little off-colour,' said Robert, 'Mr Pasty face!' pinching James on the cheek. Usually, James would respond with a similar jibe, calling him 'Beanpole', or 'Stick Insect', or something similar, but today he just brushed James's hand away and carried on looking out of the window.

'Shush,' whispered Lucy with a worried look towards the receptionist, 'They might stop us going if they think you're ill.' All the other children going home for Easter had already left, and the receptionist, Mary Rodgers, was trying to look as though she was doing some work on the computer, but secretly she was comparing prices of handbags on the internet and was not paying much attention to Lucy, Robert and James. She frowned as the door seemed to blow open in the wind but returned to her computer as it closed again.

Robert gazed out of the window. The reception room was in one of the buildings bordering a square they all referred to as 'the Quad'.

At the far end of the Quad, he could see a rectangle of green in the space between two of the buildings; the school playing fields. He would much rather be there instead of cooped up in this room. His attention was grabbed by the sight of someone he didn't recognise, wearing a tracksuit in the school colours, running on the field. What seemed unusual was that, rather than running around the perimeter of the field, as the students usually did when training, this person was running in a straight line towards the edge of the field.

Just then, a taxi drew up outside. The children had been hoping that Uncle Archie would be arriving in his vintage sports car, but there were no other passengers in the taxi. Even so, to relieve the tedium of waiting, they positioned themselves so they could watch the taxi driver as he strode towards the receptionist, presented his identification card, and handed her an envelope. It was a very official-looking envelope, with a red wax seal on the back, so Mary studied it for a few moments before opening it. Inside there was a letter, which the receptionist read, and another envelope. Then Mary consulted her computer screen before nodding to the Taxi driver and beckoning towards the children.

'Right, you Baxter children,' she said, 'This letter is from your Uncle. He had already warned us by letter that if he was delayed, he would send this taxi service to collect you. It's on our system.' She pointed to the computer screen. 'So it means you can go now... Oh, and this other envelope is for you.'

Finally, the taxi passed through the school gates, drove

through the town and headed in the direction of Cambridge. Lucy, sitting between her two brothers, studied the envelope. Like the first envelope, it had a red wax seal on the back, and this time they could see that the initials A.B. had been pressed into the seal whilst it was still wet.

'Archie Baxter!' exclaimed Lucy. She carefully opened it and read out the hand-written letter:

'My dearest children, please accept my utmost apologies for not being there in person to meet you. The fact that you are reading this means that, unfortunately, I have been delayed by circumstances beyond my control. I feared this might happen and therefore have made arrangements. I hope to be with you as soon as possible, but in the meantime, my housekeeper, Mrs Simpson, will be there to meet you in Cambridge. I am sure that you will have all that you need. Once again, my humble apologies, your Uncle Archie.'

***

After what seemed an age, the children finally clambered out of the taxi. James had slept most of the way. Robert had attempted to do some homework, not caring if his handwriting was nothing more than a scrawl. He didn't want to waste his Easter holiday doing homework, so thought he might be able to get it out of the way on the journey. Lucy would never have handed in homework that looked as scruffy as Robert's and passed the time working on a crossword puzzle that she had saved specifically for the journey. Although the youngest of the three, she was by far the cleverest of them, and she loved all kinds of puzzles. In fact, she had bought two puzzle books for her holiday and, although she was sure that she had them both with her in the School Reception, she could only find one now. She suspected that James had hidden it somewhere, but he denied it with such conviction that she almost believed him!

Finally, the taxi wove its way through the Cambridge traffic and pulled into Huskisson Street. They looked up at the brass plaque on the wall of the tall, elegant Georgian townhouse before them.

'The Baxter Museum of Curious Antiquities (Open by Appointment).'

The taxi driver slammed the boot door shut after lifting out the children's bags and muttered to no one in particular:

'Thanks for your help!'

Just then, the door to the museum opened, and Mrs Simpson, the housekeeper, rushed down the steps.

'Welcome,' she beamed, 'You must be Lucy, Robert and James. Come on up.'

'I haven't actually seen Mr Baxter for a few days,' said Mrs Simpson later, as she handed round a plate of sandwiches, 'but that's nothing unusual. I see him going off to the office at the back of the museum, and then I might not see him again for days. He doesn't like me to clean in there, so I don't know what he gets up to – labelling all his precious antiques, I suppose! The museum isn't open to the general public; people have to make an appointment. Generally, it's just dusty old professors who come; some of them look older than the exhibits!' Mrs Simpson laughed and then almost choked as she tried to eat a sandwich and laugh at the same time. 'Anyway, your rooms are ready; help yourself to anything from the fridge. I've got a flat on the top floor so if there is anything you need just give me a shout. I'll be back down to cook a meal this evening. If you want to go out, don't forget to take the key.' She pointed to a large bunch of keys hanging on the back of the kitchen door. 'Or if you want, whilst you wait for Mr Baxter, you might like to explore the museum. It's all on the floor below.'

Half an hour later, they had unpacked and were wandering around the museum. It consisted of three large rooms, with glass display cases fixed to the walls and dark polished oak cabinets below, each containing a dozen drawers, labelled with an unlikely set of topics.

'Dentistry!' exclaimed Robert, pulling out one of the drawers. Then as he saw rows of tools, from pliers and pincers to tiny saws, he shuddered and quickly pushed it back.

'Noses!' laughed Lucy, and she pulled out a drawer to reveal a collection of false noses, from realistic medical ones to big red clown noses.

Eventually, the children found themselves in the third room. Like the other two rooms, it was lined with display cases, but this time the window had become part of the display; the floor-to-ceiling window looked over a small, walled back garden but was partly obscured by dozens of kites which were suspended from the ceiling, and which appeared to dance before their eyes.

'Indian Fighting Kite,' read James. 'This one's from Korea, and that big one's from Japan! 'On the side wall, there was a door marked 'Private'.

'Oh, this won't mean us,' said James, who, even though he wasn't feeling well, hadn't lost his inquisitive nature, 'we are family. This must be Uncle Archie's office.' He turned the handle and swung the door open. The office was smaller than the children had expected. It was dark, as there wasn't a window, and it was dusty, presumably because Mrs Simpson wasn't allowed to clean it. There was a single desk piled high with cardboard boxes, and at the far end of the room, there was a bookcase stacked floor to ceiling with ancient leather-bound books. Lucy wrinkled her nose.

'I can't see why anyone would want to spend time in here,' she said. 'Come on, let's go.'

'I'm sure Mr Baxter will be back in time for dinner,' said Mrs Simpson as she lifted pan lids, checking on the progress of her cooking. Lucy was standing at the bay window looking up and down the street. From her position, she had a clear view of the front door. James and Robert were sprawled in front of the TV, taking full advantage of the fact that they were alone and could decide which channel they wanted to watch without the arguments that would break out whenever anyone tried to change channels on the TV at school. Suddenly, the door burst open and there stood Uncle Archie, arms outstretched, with a wide grin on his face.

'Uncle Archie,' squealed Lucy, 'I didn't see you arrive.' She rushed over to him just as James and Robert arrived. Archie clasped them all to him, he was a big, dishevelled looking man, and he easily wrapped his arms around all three of them.

'You're here! You're here!'

Later, after Archie had apologised for the umpteenth time for not being able to meet them at the school, they were all sitting around the dining table catching up with their news.

'There's not a lot to tell,' said Robert, 'it's just school! I made the school rugby team, though. We've only lost one match, and our coach said I should do well in the athletics season next term. I'm one of the fastest runners in the year, and I came second in the County cross-country running competition. Oh, and I'm captain of the cricket team.'

'Well, that's great news,' said Archie, 'and James, are

you a sportsman too?' James shook his head.

'Oh, I'm not bad,' said James 'I can hold my own, but it's drama that I really like. I had the leading part in a Shakespeare play, Hamlet, last term. You'll have to come and see me next term. We're putting on Under Milk Wood by Dylan Thomas.'

Archie nodded.

'I will certainly try my best; I've just got to finish a project that I am working on…' His voice trailed off for a moment, and a worried look flashed across his face, then just as quickly, it was gone, replaced with the big grin and twinkling eyes that they had come to expect from Uncle Archie. 'Lucy!' he exclaimed, 'how about you?'

'Well,' replied Lucy, 'I'm not the sporty type, and I don't think I'll ever make a good actress, but I'm doing well with my lessons, especially Maths, and I'm in the Chess club.'

'She's always doing puzzles,' chipped in James.

'Well, that's good,' replied Archie, 'I can't tell you any details because it's all hush hush top secret, but when I worked for the government, I was a Code Breaker. Do you know what that is?' James shook his head.

'Well, when one spy wants to leave a message for another, they write it in a way that looks like gobbledygook. Each letter or number is substituted for another.' He thought for a moment, then scribbled something down on a piece of paper. 'See if you can crack that. In the meantime, I've got something to finish off in my office. I'll be back up in a couple of hours.'

It didn't take long for Robert and James to lose interest, but Lucy took the piece of paper over to a seat by the window and stared intently at it, chewing a pencil as she tried to puzzle it out.

ARCHIE
BAXTER
DPYN-5773
ORLIZ - 5778
EKAIEH – 5778

An hour later, Lucy marched triumphantly into the lounge, waving the piece of paper in the air.

'Got it!' she exclaimed, 'Well, not all of it, but enough to get the general idea. See, I wondered why Uncle Archie had written his name at the top, and then it dawned on me. That's the code. You substitute the letters in the second line for those in the top line. So an A becomes a B, and an R becomes an A and a C becomes an X. Then I looked at the three lines below and substituted the letters I knew, and after that it was easy!'

'Yeah, yeah, easy!' chorused her brothers. They were trying to peer around her so as not to miss any of the football match they were watching on the TV.

'Yes,' continued Lucy, 'I wondered what the significance of the following lines was, four letters, then five letters, then six, and then I spotted it; they're our names! Now look at the numbers, they must be the years we were born: see, both yours are the same numbers, whereas mine has the last number different because I'm a year younger.'

'Yeah, yeah, easy!' repeated Robert and James. Lucy looked up from the paper and, seeing Robert and James were not the slightest bit interested in her discovery and were more intent on watching the football, she grabbed a couple of cushions and flung them at her brothers before storming out of the room.

'You two are impossible!'

***

Over the next few days, life at the museum apartment settled into a pattern. Uncle Archie tended to come and go, although he was sometimes there at breakfast time. The children tended not to get up at any regular time, a welcome change from the strict rigours of school life.

'Are you sure you wouldn't like me to arrange more things for you to do?' Archie had asked one evening, scratching at a newly emerging beard. 'I've got such a lot of work to do at the moment, but I could ask Mrs Simpson to accompany you.'

'Oh no, we're quite happy just mooching about,' replied Robert.

'We can find our own way around Cambridge; it's not far to the shops,' said Lucy. 'We are not looking for adventure; a change is as good as a rest!'

So the children mostly divided their time between watching TV and wandering around the city centre. When the boys turned the television to the sports channel, which was a frequent occurrence, Lucy would curl up on the chair in the bay window with her puzzle book. Sometimes, when the sun was shining, she would sit out in the back garden. It was a little overgrown.

'It hasn't had its normal spruce-up,' Uncle Archie had explained, 'because Bert the gardener broke his leg, but he'll be back soon.'

Mrs Simpson cooked them meals at lunchtime and in the evening. One evening Archie came in for dinner clutching a notebook.

'My, your beard grows fast,' said Mrs Simpson as she put the plates on the table. 'If you don't mind me saying so, it looks like you could do with a little trim! Oh, you've cut yourself,' she said, pointing to Archie's cheek, 'well you've certainly not done it shaving,' and that set her off on one of her laughter attacks.

'Hmmph!' snorted Archie. Then he turned his attention to the children. He spent the whole evening gathering information: 'Just a little research I'm carrying out, statistics and data and such like. Some of this I know, but I just want to check.' It was certainly thorough: from information about the times of day when they were born, through to their current weight and height and even their shoe sizes. He produced a tape measure and recorded the size of their heads, the length of their noses, the distance between their eyes. He even asked them to place both hands on a page in his book, and he drew around their outline. It was all very good-humoured until James let it slip that he hadn't been feeling his usual self.

'I can't put my finger on it,' said James. 'At first, I felt unwell, kind of weak and sick, but now that's passed, and now I just feel kind of distant.'

'I had noticed your complexion had changed,' said Lucy 'I mean, you're always paler than the two of us, I think with having red hair, but tonight you look even paler than normal, even translucent.'

'Yeah, you look like one of those fish at the bottom of a very deep dark ocean that never see the sun,' laughed Robert. Archie's mood instantly changed, and the face that had previously been roaring with laughter now was one of frowning anxiety.

'Oh, I was worried about this,' he muttered. 'Oh, I've so much to do, so far to go.' With that, he snapped his notebook shut and rushed out of the room, heading to his office in the Museum.

***

Lucy began to notice that Archie's behaviour was becoming more and more erratic. She bought a notebook and started to record her thoughts. Things came to a head a few days later, after Lucy had spent the afternoon baking. With expert guidance from Mrs Simpson, she had baked a delicious Victoria Sponge cake. She knew that Uncle Archie would be down in his office because he had rushed upstairs fifteen minutes before the cake was ready to collect something from his room. Lucy cut a slice of cake and went downstairs to the office. When she got there, she found the office door locked and the museum empty. Puzzled, she returned to the kitchen, only to hear, a few moments later, the sound of Uncle Archie's footsteps running up the stairs to his room, then returning downstairs.

'Uncle Archie!' she cried. But Archie was in too much of a hurry and didn't hear her as he clattered back down the stairs. So Lucy went back to the kitchen, cut another piece of cake (as James had eaten the one that she had cut previously), and went back downstairs to the office. This time the office door wasn't locked. However, when she knocked and then looked inside, she found to her surprise that the office was empty. She was certain Uncle Archie hadn't gone outside, she would have heard the heavy oak door slamming shut, and she could see that he was not in the museum. Once again, she returned to the kitchen carrying a piece of cake, only this time she was even more perplexed.

The following day, after breakfast, when Archie bounded down the stairs to the office, Lucy rushed to the bay window from where she knew she could see the front door. After a few moments, she was reassured that Archie had not left the house, so she rushed downstairs through the museum to the office. She wasn't quite sure what she would say when she saw Archie but thought she could ask him something about secret codes. Again Lucy was disappointed. The office door was locked. This time she hammered on it, but there was no answer from Uncle Archie.

'We need to have a meeting,' announced Lucy to Robert & James, 'Please come with me to the garden,'

'But we're watching the television,' complained Robert.

'You're always watching the television,' retorted Lucy, 'This is important.'

Five minutes later, Robert and James were seated on the garden bench. The expressions on their faces clearly indicated that they would rather be somewhere else.

Lucy checked over her shoulder for anyone eavesdropping, thereby adding to the sense of mystery.

'Something strange is going on,' she whispered, 'It's about Uncle Archie. 'Have you wondered where he goes when he's not with us?'

'He goes to his office,' replied James, 'He told us he had lots of work to do.'

'Well, that's what I thought,' said Lucy, and she described what had happened when she tried to give him a piece of cake.

'Maybe he has to go out sometimes,' said Robert.

'I thought of that too, but you can see the front door from the seat in the window upstairs, and I've never seen him leave the house, and look!' (she gestured to the back door.) 'It's all overgrown by the back door because the gardener has a broken leg; that door hasn't been opened for months!'

'I don't know,' said James, 'Maybe there is a secret tunnel.'

'Yes, that could be it.' said Lucy.' Another thing, though, have you noticed something strange about Uncle Archie's beard? Sometimes it's quite long and bushy, and sometimes it's shorter and neater.'

'Well, he probably trims it then,' replied Robert.

'But it can be short in the morning, then long in the evening. Surely a beard can't grow that fast?' said Lucy.

"Do you think it's a false beard?' asked Robert.

'Surely it would be the same length all the time if it was false. Anyway, it doesn't look false,' said James.

'There's another thing, and I have only just thought of this,' said Lucy, 'Look at the windows.' The children looked up. The back was less majestic than the front of the house, being built in red brick rather than in stone, but the house still retained that elegant sense of symmetry common to all Georgian houses. 'See, there's the museum window, with all the kites hanging in the window, and there, next to it, is where the office is.'

'Yes. So?'

'But don't you remember, there isn't a window in the office, it's quite a small room. So which room is that window in?' said Lucy, pointing to the window on the left-hand side. Although it was a ground floor window at the back of the house, the windows were quite high up. Too high to see into and, in any case, the interior was obscured by close-fitting wooden shutters.

'Let's go exploring tomorrow,' said Robert, 'You know Lucy, you are right; it's all very odd.'

Little were the children to know, but the following day things were going to get even stranger.

CHAPTER TWO

James didn't sleep well that night. He woke up in the middle of the night feeling hot and thirsty. He quietly tiptoed along the hallway to the kitchen to get a drink of orange juice from the fridge. He didn't bother turning the light on because he could see from the light of the fridge. He noticed as he reached in to get the carton of juice that his hand looked even paler than usual, almost transparent, but he put it down to a combination of tiredness and the poor light. He stumbled back to bed and was soon asleep, only to wake up again an hour later. He was thankful that he was not sharing a room with Robert, as he would have disturbed his brother's sleep. This time, James decided to turn on the light and read for a little. He reached over for his copy of Under Milk Wood; maybe he could do something useful and learn his part for the school play. As he clasped the tatty school book, he gave a gasp and almost dropped it. His hand was definitely transparent. Not completely clear, he could see a kind of mist-coloured shape where his hand was, but he could also see right through it so that he could read the title of the play beneath.

James sat back to gather his thoughts.

'Am I dead? Is this what happens when you die? No, I'm holding a book,' James threw it up in the air and caught it.

'Surely I couldn't do that if I had died. Maybe I'm a ghost or a poltergeist! But I don't believe in ghosts. How could I be something that I don't believe in? I know; I'm asleep. All this is just a dream. If I pinch myself, I will wake up.'

James pinched himself as hard as he could.

'Ow! Well, I'm sure I'm not a ghost. I don't think you can hurt a ghost by pinching it, but I'm not sure how to prove to myself that this isn't a dream, even though my arm really hurts.'

James had a mixture of emotions, he was worried about his condition, but increasingly he was getting more curious and excited. He jumped up and went over to the mirror to see if his whole body was affected. It was; he could barely see himself in the reflection. Not only that, he was wearing pyjamas, and they, too, were transparent. He took his pyjama top off and placed it on the bed, and gradually, over a period of two or three minutes, it returned to its normal colour.

'Interesting, very interesting,' he said out loud. Then he reached for his favourite T-shirt, put it on, and watched in the mirror as the colour slowly drained away from it.

'Zat iz very interesting!' he said, using one of the funny

voices that would invariably make his friends laugh in class. Then he had a thought. 'Talking! Surely that could prove something. He picked up his mobile phone and then paused whilst he wondered who he could telephone at this time of the night.

'I know.' He reached for his jeans because he remembered there was a leaflet for a nearby 24-hour pizza place in the pocket.

'Georgio's Pizzas,' said a weary voice over the phone.

'Hello, can you hear me?'

'Yes, mate, it's a phone, you speak, and I listen.'

'You are sure you can hear me?'

'Look, do you want a Pizza or not? '

'Well, I'm not really hungry.' The line went quiet as Giorgio hung up. Clearly, he wasn't in the mood for a chat!

James went back to the mirror. To his amazement, he was now completely invisible! He rushed into Robert's room.

'Robert, wake up, look at me, I'm invisible,' then he giggled, 'No, you can't look at me because I am invisible.'

'What time is it?' groaned Robert.

'I don't know, maybe five o'clock.'

'Go away, James. I'm not in the mood.' It was never easy to wake Robert.

'But Robert…'

'Go away!'

James retreated. He doubted if Robert had even opened his eyes. He was buzzing with excitement, though. He had to do something. He could have some fun! James dashed back into his room and threw on some warm clothes, pausing in front of the mirror to watch them disappear. In the hallway, he noticed that Uncle Archie's door was slightly ajar. He slowly pushed it open and peered around it. To his surprise, he saw that the room was empty. The bed hadn't been slept in. He decided to investigate further and went down the stairs to see if Archie was in his office. The door was locked. James knocked; he wasn't surprised when there was no answer because he would have expected to see the light shining beneath the door if Uncle Archie had been there.

James bounded back up the stairs and grabbed the big bunch of keys from the back of the kitchen door. He scrawled a note on an old envelope:

'*Gone out, back later, James*' and left it on the kitchen table. He had money in his pocket. He considered going back for his phone then remembered the battery was almost dead. Now he felt ready for adventure and leapt down the steps two at a time. He unlocked the big oak front door, locked it behind him, posted the keys back through the letterbox in case anyone else needed them, and stepped out into the road. Dawn was breaking, the birds were starting to sing, and James was starting the most remarkable day of his life so far.

There were very few people up; it was still early. Occasionally, there was a light on in someone's house. He could hear the sound of a car passing by a few streets away, but the road he was walking along was quiet. Then suddenly, the silence was broken by the sound of the milkman, who drove around the corner, parked his milk float, then sprinted up the steps of the houses, leaving bottles of milk and collecting the empties. James suffered a moment of nerves; he still didn't believe that he was invisible, so he stopped in front of the milk float and smiled at the milkman. Surely he would see him, but no, the milkman walked past him missing him by a few inches as he clattered the empty milk bottles into a crate, climbed into his van and moved on up the road. James had to jump out of the way of the milk float as it passed, confirming not only that he was invisible, but also it served as a warning that he had better be careful when he crossed the road!

At the end of the road, he had a choice, either he could turn right and walk down to the City Centre, with its historic University buildings and quaint shops, or he could turn left and walk to the modern shopping mall. James decided to visit the shopping mall. On his way, he passed Georgio's Pizza parlour and noticed a glum-looking young man reading a newspaper at the counter. Surely this was the same person James had spoken to earlier. He couldn't resist pushing open the door. The man looked up, presuming the wind had blown the door open, then, because he couldn't be bothered to get up and close it, he returned to his newspaper.

'Are you sure you can hear me?' whispered James.

'You again,' snarled the man, jumping over to the telephone; he presumed he had left it on 'speaker phone'. He frowned with puzzlement when he picked the phone up, heard the dialling tone, and realised no one was on the other end. He didn't even notice the door close as James, suppressing a giggle, slipped out of the shop.

James had to wait a while before the shopping mall opened as it was still early, but eventually, a security guard arrived with a big bunch of keys and unlocked the entrance. James followed one of the shop assistants into the mall, taking care not to bump into her as they negotiated their way through the revolving door. After wandering from shop to shop, James came to the conclusion that, as he didn't particularly like going shopping when he was visible, it wasn't any more enjoyable when he was invisible. He thought it would be fun to play some tricks. There was a

shop assistant hanging clothes on a rack, making sure that
all the colours were coordinated so, when James was sure
no one could see, he mixed up the colours. But it wasn't
fun at all; it just seemed cruel. All he was doing was creating
extra work for someone. James knew he had a reputation
for being a joker, but he realised then that he needed an
audience. Then, to his horror, he remembered that there
would be security cameras in the store. What if the cameras
had caught the clothes mysteriously moving about on film?
James rushed out towards the entrance of the shop.

The shop was getting quite busy now. There were two
young men out shopping with their girlfriends on the route
to the entrance. They weren't together; in fact, Jak and
Wayne hadn't even noticed each other, as they were
standing back-to-back a few feet apart, but both were
feeling fed up at being dragged out to go shopping early in
the morning. James tried to slip between them, but, at that
moment, each stepped back slightly, and James tumbled
into both of them.

'Oy! Watch it,' said Jak.

'You watch it, you clumsy oaf,' replied Wayne.

'Who are you calling a clumsy oaf?'

'What's going on?' shouted one of the girls.

'It's 'im. He kicked me.'

'No I didn't; you knocked into me!'

Luckily, there was a security guard close by who
rushed over and managed to calm the two men down
before the situation escalated. James carefully picked
himself up and crept out of the store. He needed time to
think things through, so he found himself a seat in an area
of the shopping mall that was a little less crowded and sat
down to ponder his future.

'Maybe I am a Superhero,' he thought. In the comic

books, the ability to become invisible would be an advantage. He would notice evil deeds being carried out and be able to step in unnoticed to save the day. As he watched the crowds of shoppers bustling backwards and forwards, he realised there were two major flaws in this idea. Firstly, there didn't seem to be anything unusual happening before his eyes. What were the chances of seeing a crime or being able to rescue someone in distress every time he went out? Secondly, he didn't think he felt brave enough to deal with a criminal anyway!

However, thinking about Superheroes did start him thinking about Good and Evil. In the wrong hands, the power to become invisible could be catastrophic for mankind. James had set out with the idea of playing a few tricks, but what if an invisible man was truly set on causing serious mischief? Perhaps an invisible man might have started out as a good person and then become embittered. James' love of drama began to take over as he envisaged the scenario of a cruel, twisted man, unloved by a society that couldn't see him, a society that felt threatened by him, a man who turned to crime in order to avenge himself. James shuddered and resolved that he shouldn't abuse his 'powers'. He had to remain on the side of 'Good.'

For a long while, James sat and watched the shoppers. Occasionally he had to jump out of his seat when someone else came to sit on it and so sat on the floor close by. It was mildly interesting listening to people's conversations. If he were a playwright, he could be writing conversations down to use in his plays. Actually, he couldn't write them down because his pencil and paper would be invisible, and he wouldn't be able to see what he was writing. He would have to record them. Then again, the conversations were all quite ordinary, just the kind of things you might hear on a bus.

'You know Shirley. I think I liked the shoes that we saw in the first shop the best.'

'I agree Gladys, I always say you can't beat quality, and they were quality.'

'You do always say that Shirley, quality you say, you can't beat quality, and they were quality! Bit pricey, though, but you have to pay for quality.'

'Do you want to try them on again?'

'No, don't think I can afford them, fancy a cup of coffee and a cake?'

As the two shoppers headed off in search of refreshment, James came to the conclusion that he was feeling hungry. After all, it was almost lunchtime now, and he hadn't had any breakfast. This presented a new problem. Where was he going to get some food from?

'I know,' he thought, 'there is a vending machine on the next floor down.'

It took longer to get there than he imagined because he didn't dare to travel on the escalator. It was too busy, so he had to weave his way across to the staircase in the centre of the mall. Finally, he stood before the vending machine. It was a sophisticated machine that would give change and accept notes too. James reached for his wallet and realised that, of course, he couldn't see what was in it. He only had a few coins and, although he could work out what they were by their size and weight, they did not total enough to buy anything. He would have to use a note. There was a diagram on the vending machine to illustrate which way up to feed the money into the slot. James would have to take a guess; there were four possible options. Checking there was no one around, James fed the money into the slot and felt the note slide between his fingers and enter the machine. He heard a whir as he waited to press the buttons to make his selection, but then disaster. He must have fed the money in the wrong way, and the noise he heard was the sound of the machine spitting out the reject note. He hadn't noticed it at first because, of course, the note was invisible, but then, just as the note regained its colour and was clearly on show hanging from the slot, a group of young teenagers raced around the corner.

'Hey, look at that! That's mine!'

'I saw it first.'

'Come on, let's split it,' and grabbing the note, they ran off laughing and joking about their good fortune. Crestfallen, James retreated. He had another note, but he didn't dare risk losing it. Even if he had managed to select something, what if someone had heard it falling into the tray? He might have lost it then anyway! James could smell food; around the corner was the Food Hall, a square where shoppers could select food from various different counters around the outside, then sit at any of the tables in the centre. There were pizzas, burgers, sandwiches, Chinese food, Mexican food, Indian food. By now, James felt ravenous. He was determined that he wouldn't be dishonest, but what about the food that people had left on their plates? That was only going to go to waste, and lots of people seemed to order much more than they could possibly eat. He circled the hall and saw one couple deep in conversation. In front of them were the remains of a plate of sandwiches, but one of them hadn't been touched. The couple got up to leave, and James slipped over to the table. He had thought of a strategy. He gently raised the sandwich slightly from the plate and, making sure the people employed to clear the tables were not nearby, he simply waited for it to disappear. He couldn't attract attention by having food flying through the air as he whisked it away from the tables. In this way, he managed to eat two sandwiches and a piece of cake before pausing and thinking, 'So it has come to this! I am having to scavenge to survive! I think it's time to go back to the Museum.'

Getting back was exhausting. The town was so busy now that James had to keep all his wits about him. People were so erratic when they walked. They would stop without warning, then suddenly change direction. Children would run in all directions. Youths would whiz by on skateboards or roller skates. Cyclists would sometimes appear without warning, weaving their way through traffic, ignoring red lights at the traffic signals, even mounting the pavement. None of this was out of the ordinary. It was just that, normally, people could see each other and avoid collisions.

Crossing the road proved tricky too. James tried mostly to use pedestrian crossing places governed by traffic lights. However, sometimes they were too busy, and he dared not risk bumping into people. He sometimes had to wait whilst the lights changed several times, pausing until just a few people were crossing, then he could tag along at the end, hoping that cyclists wouldn't jump the lights thinking the road was clear. It dawned on James that he would be in serious trouble if he were to be hit by a car: no one would know he was there. Even if someone found him, what could a doctor or a surgeon do for a patient they couldn't see?

At last, James arrived at Huskisson Street; he was almost back at the Museum, and he thought of another potential hazard if he wanted to remain undetected; rain! He could feel a few spots of rain on his face. He held out a hand and saw a drop of rain appear to stop in mid-air, then trickle around the contour of his fingers before vanishing. If it were to rain heavily, he would present an unusual sight to any passers-by.

The Museum door was locked, so he pressed hard on the bell, stood to one side and waited. Mrs Simpson came to the door, but she didn't open it fully, she just peered around the door and, seeing no one there, she muttered 'Blooming kids!' and closed it again.

James couldn't think of anything to do other than ring it again. The same thing happened.

'Think I've got nothing better to do than run up and down stairs,' complained Mrs Simpson, closing the door again. James tried a third time. Luckily this time, Mrs Simpson opened the door wide.

'If I get hold of you....!' she shouted as she came down the steps looking for the mischievous children that she thought were playing tricks on her. In the meantime, James slipped through the door and bounded up the stairs to Uncle Archie's apartment. There was no one else there. James was so relieved to be back in the safety of the apartment that he almost felt like crying. He also felt incredibly tired. Not only had the day's events been exhausting, both physically and mentally, but also, he had not had much sleep the night before. James realised that the best place he could be was in his own bed; he climbed in, drew the covers over his head and almost immediately was fast asleep.

CHAPTER THREE

Earlier, whilst James had been exploring the shopping centre in a state of invisibility, Robert and Lucy had sat down for breakfast with Uncle Archie.

'Do you know where James has gone,' asked Archie, waving the note that James had left. 'It just says *Gone out, back later, James*'

'No,' replied Robert. 'He's a real pest. He woke me up in the middle of the night.'

'Did he,' asked Lucy 'What was he doing?'

'He came into my room saying he was invisible.'

'What!' exploded Archie, 'Invisible? Are you sure?'

'Oh, it's just James being James,' replied Robert. 'I didn't even open my eyes.'

'He's always playing tricks,' said Lucy.

'Oh no!' groaned Archie, 'It's all happening too fast, and I haven't got much time. Look, I've got some things to talk about with you. It's very, very important. We all have to meet up, say at 7.00 pm. Don't be late. Right now, it's even more crucial that I get on with something.'

With that, and without even waiting to finish his breakfast, he rushed into his room and then almost immediately rushed out again.

'Don't forget, 7.00 o'clock!' he shouted as he ran down the stairs.

Lucy sprang from her chair and rushed out to the hallway. Peering over the bannister rail, she was just in time to see Archie entering the museum. As fast as she could, she sped down the stairs, silently following Archie into the museum. He had already left the first room, but she could hear his footsteps as he approached the office at the rear of the building. Lucy tiptoed through the museum rooms and heard the sound of Archie opening the office door and then shutting it behind him. She crouched behind a display case in the final room from where she had a good view of the office door. She could hear Archie moving around inside, and she could see that the light was on because it shone through the gap beneath the door. There were some odd scraping noises. Then, to her surprise, she saw the light click off. Surely it was too dark in there to work as there was no window in that room? Lucy thought about the window that they had seen from the garden the day before.

'There must be a secret way into another room,' she thought. She hurried out of the museum rooms back to the hallway. She noticed the bunch of keys that James had posted through the letterbox still lying on the doormat 'Good. I don't have to go upstairs for them.' Snatching them up, she ran out of the house and then through the side gate into the back garden. Looking up, she could see there was a light on in the mystery room. So that proved it. That's where Uncle Archie was. Then that light clicked off too. It could be because it was full daylight now, and maybe Uncle Archie did not need the light on to work. Or maybe Uncle Archie had come back out of that room. She dashed back to the front door; he couldn't have reached that door before her, so he must still be inside. As she turned the key in the front door and opened it, she half expected to see him on his way out, but he wasn't there. Nor was he in any of the museum rooms, and the office was in darkness. Lucy slowly turned the door handle; it was locked. She tried to look through the keyhole, but it was too dark.

Lucy had another idea. She dashed back up to her room, taking the steps two at a time, grabbed her school bag and rushed back to the office door. She was sure she had been so quick that it was unlikely that she had missed anyone coming out of the museum. She found a roll of clear sticky tape in her bag and a pair of scissors. She cut a tiny sliver of tape and fastened it high up, so half of it stuck to the door and the other half to the door frame. Now, if anyone came in or out of the door, she would be able to tell if the tape had been disturbed. It was so small that it would be extremely unlikely that anyone would notice it. There was nothing else to do but return to the apartment. Robert was still sitting at the breakfast table, oblivious to all her exertions.

'Where have you been?' he asked.

'Looking for Uncle Archie. He didn't come back up here, did he?'

Robert shook his head.

'Come on; let's have a look in his bedroom,' she replied, 'We've got around fifteen minutes before Mrs

Simpson comes down to start tidying and cleaning.'

The room was quite unremarkable. It was very similar in size to their bedrooms. The bed covers were all ruffled up. There was a book about Ancient Greece on the bedside table. Robert opened the large double wardrobe.

'Look at this,' he exclaimed. The clothes on one side were quite ordinary, the clothes that they were used to seeing Uncle Archie wearing. Not especially fashionable, but clothes that wouldn't date. However, the other side of the wardrobe looked like the rail from a fancy dress shop! There was such a mixture of styles: a pin-striped city suit, a chef's outfit, a military general's uniform as well as an ordinary soldier's uniform, even a velvet cloak together with a bejewelled crown hanging next to a scruffy set of clothes that the average tramp wouldn't wear.

'We had better get going,' said Lucy, 'Mrs Simpson will be here in a minute.

Back in her favourite window seat, Lucy recounted to Robert how she had followed Uncle Archie to his office and how she thought that either he was either still working in a secret room or that there was a secret way outside from that room. The clothes were a puzzle.

'They're not exactly disguises,' said Robert, 'I mean, it wouldn't be much of a disguise walking about dressed as a king!

'Maybe he's an actor,' said Lucy. Just then, Mrs Simpson came into the room to start cleaning it.

'Mrs Simpson,' said Lucy, 'Does Uncle Archie act in plays or films?'

'Funny you should say that,' replied Mrs Simpson, 'He says he's interested in amateur dramatics, and he's got lots of funny costumes in his wardrobe, but I've never seen him in anything. Well, he's not invited me to see anything;

maybe that shows you how good an actor he is. Maybe he's got stage fright!' and she erupted into one of her laughing fits.

After that Robert and Lucy were at a loss about what to do.

'Well, it's all a bit of a mystery,' said Robert, 'but maybe it will all be a lot clearer after this meeting with Uncle Archie tonight.'

'Why don't we go into town and see if we can see James?' said Lucy. 'Anyway, I want to buy a new puzzle book. That second book of mine never turned up.'

'Can't see why you need to buy a puzzle book,' said Robert 'We've got enough puzzles happening right here. But yes, let's go and see if we can find James.'

They didn't realise it, but even if James had still been at the mall, they wouldn't have been able to see him. They sat in the food hall eating salad and chips; if they had been there an hour earlier, they might have noticed a sandwich on the empty table next to them mysteriously vanishing before their eyes.

Later, having looked in all the places, they thought James likely to be, they returned to the museum in Huskisson St. Lucy looked around James's bedroom door. James, although still fast asleep, had been quite restless and had kicked off his covers, so what Lucy saw was just a rumpled unmade bed.

'That's funny,' she thought. 'Usually, Mrs Simpson makes the beds in the morning. She must have forgotten'. What she didn't realise, of course, was that James had got back into bed after Mrs Simpson had tidied his room.

James woke up about an hour later. He checked in the mirror; he was still completely invisible. He could hear the sound of the television, so he tiptoed to the lounge door.

As expected, Robert was watching the sports channel, and Lucy was curled up in her window seat with a puzzle book.

'What shall I do?' he thought. 'How shall I tell them without scaring them too much?' He had an idea. James returned to his bedroom, climbed into bed, and pulled the covers right over himself.

'Hey guys!' he shouted. 'Lucy, Robert. Can you come to my room a moment?'

'He's back,' said Lucy as she jumped up, 'That's funny; I didn't see him come in.'

'I can't believe how lazy you are,' said Robert angrily as they entered the bedroom. 'In bed! Where have you been? We were worried about you.'

'I'm sorry,' came the muffled voice beneath the bed covers. 'I've got something important to tell you, something rather scary. I tried to tell you last night … I really am invisible.' Very slowly, James pulled back the covers. Instead of the gasp of astonishment that he had expected, they just laughed.

'Oh James!' said Robert, 'Typical! How's it done? Do you pull the covers with strings?' Lucy approached the bed, waving her hands about, expecting to feel tiny threads attached to the sheets. Robert looked around the room to see where James was hiding. Then Lucy screamed; she had felt James's outstretched leg.

'I told you, it's true,' said James, 'I am invisible.' Only Robert heard this, though, because Lucy had fainted and was sprawled across the bed, trapping James underneath her.

Ten minutes later, after washing her face with cold water, Lucy had regained her composure, and James recounted the events of the day. He was always good at telling stories, a reason why he was so good at drama, but the tale he had to tell was so incredible that his audience was spellbound. Finally, Robert spoke.

'I'm sorry I told you to go away last night. It's both amazing and extremely worrying.'

'Apart from the dangers if you were ever injured, just imagine what would happen if the newspapers found out about it,' said Lucy. 'The street would be full of reporters and photographers and TV cameras. They would never leave you alone.'

'I know. Well, I wouldn't be very photogenic; you two would feel the brunt of it.'

'And then what would happen if the government found out? They would take you away. You would spend your whole life having tests done on you by doctors. And I bet the military people would get involved. They would be interested in trying to make invisible armies.'

'We have to keep this a secret for the moment,' said Lucy. 'We'll only tell Uncle Archie. He seemed very concerned about your note. Maybe he knows something about it. Anyway, he wants to see us at 7.00 o'clock. He has something important to tell us.'

'There's not much call for invisible actors,' moaned James. Then, with a smile that no one could see. he quipped, 'Well, not on TV or in the movies, I'll have to concentrate on a career in radio!'

At six o'clock, Mrs Simpson came downstairs to prepare the evening meal.

'I presume James came back?'

'Oh yes,' said Robert, 'He's in his room.'

'Your Uncle said he would be back for seven o'clock' she said, 'So I'm putting these potatoes in the oven to bake. They will be ready by then. All you have to do is put these pizzas in the oven,' she gestured towards the kitchen workbench. 'They will take ten minutes; put them directly on the shelf, you don't need a baking tray…here's me presuming you can't read the instructions on the packaging with all your fancy education,' she laughed, 'I'll just do a salad then I'll go on upstairs. Don't forget to turn the oven off!'

Mrs Simpson left after ten minutes, promising to return at eight o'clock to tidy up the kitchen. It seemed a long wait. They were hoping for the answers to so many questions. They carried out Mrs Simpson's instructions, and at seven o'clock, the meal was ready.

'Well, we may as well eat ours now,' said Robert fifteen minutes later. Archie still hadn't come. 'No point in our pizza getting cold.' It was an eerie sight sitting next to James and watching the food fly up into the air and disappear as James wolfed it down. He was glad of the opportunity to sit and eat in comfort after his experiences in the Food Hall. With just ten minutes to go before Mrs Simpson came down, they made a decision.

'We'll wrap up Uncle Archie's slice of pizza and take it down to him. We can't risk Mrs Simpson finding out about James just yet.' said Robert.

'I'll write a note saying: "We've all gone down to the office", which will be the truth,' said Lucy.

'If I mess up Uncle Archie's plate, she will think he's with us,' said James. As he spoke, the remaining clean knife and fork danced in the air, smearing a small piece of pizza across Uncle Archie's plate. Whilst Robert wrapped up the rest of the pizza in a piece of tinfoil, Lucy grabbed a notebook and pen from her room. Hopefully, Uncle Archie would be telling them important information and, being the organised one out of the three; she wanted to make sure she wrote it all down.

***

'Look,' said Lucy, pointing to the sticky tape she had fastened to the door, 'no one has been in or out of the room since this morning. I know that Uncle Archie went in and then through to a secret room at the back, and I don't think he came out of this door before I managed to put this tape there.'

'So either he is still in there, or there's another way out,' said Robert. They banged on the door, but there was no answer. It was still locked.

'Do you think Uncle Archie may have had some kind of accident?' asked Lucy, 'He might be ill or something, waiting for someone to rescue him.' Lucy fished a miniature flashlight out of her bag and shone it through the keyhole.

'The key is in the lock,' said Lucy.

'I know!' said Robert, pulling a penknife out of his pocket. 'Have you got a big piece of paper in your bag, Lucy?'

'Just this,' said Lucy, holding up her notebook.

'I'll get a newspaper,' said James, 'won't be a moment.'

'Be careful!'

James crept back into the apartment. Mrs Simpson was singing to herself as she cleared away the dishes. James found the previous day's newspaper on the table in the lounge and held it for a few minutes until it slowly vanished from sight. He then sauntered past Mrs Simpson, even popping a cherry tomato from the salad into his mouth whilst her back was turned, and then ran back downstairs where Robert and Lucy were waiting anxiously.

'I'm back,' said James. Lucy jumped. Even though she was expecting him, the sound of his voice coming out of thin air was very strange. James laid the newspaper on the floor and stepped back.

'You just have to wait,' he said, and sure enough, gradually, the colour flooded back into the newspaper. Robert unfolded it and then pushed a sheet of newspaper under the door. Then, using his penknife, he pushed the key out of the lock, and it clattered onto the newspaper behind.

'Saw this on a film,' he said proudly as he pulled the newspaper back from under the door and held up the big iron key. Quickly they unlocked the door and stepped into the office.

'Are you in yet, James?' asked Lucy.

'Yes,' came a voice from the corner of the room. James was getting used to the idea of keeping out of the way. Lucy turned on the light and closed the door.

'Don't touch anything yet,' said Lucy, 'Let's just look.'

The room seemed unchanged from when they last saw it. On the left was the large mahogany desk on which an assortment of cardboard boxes was piled high. Each had a tightly fitting lid and had a handwritten label stuck on the side.

'Roman coins; Victorian lace hankies; Bronze age bracelets; Elizabethan cutlery,' read James, using a voice more suitable for TV quiz presenters listing the prizes to be won.'

There were more similar boxes piled up on the floor on the right-hand side. All the boxes were covered in a fine layer of dust.

'I don't think anyone has touched these boxes for a long while,' said Robert, 'We would see fingerprints in the dust!'

'There's definitely not a doorway in the walls either side,' said Lucy, 'So there must be a secret door in the bookcase!'

They all moved closer. The bookcase was made of a heavy, dark wood and divided into five sections. Floor to ceiling were rows of books. They were leather-bound and ancient, with embossed covers and gilt lettering. Some were brown; others were green, red or blue. These weren't the kind of books that some people have in their bookcases just for show. They were well-used; the covers were split and scuffed, the colour worn through here and there. Some of the lettering had worn off. Where to start?

Robert pulled the chair from behind the desk over to the bookcase and stood on it. Like everything else in the room, the bookcase was covered in a fine layer of dust. Now that Robert had a higher vantage point, he noticed that there was one section of shelf that was not dusty. One of the books on a high shelf must have been taken out recently because the wood in front of it was clean and shiny. Robert pulled the book out, and there behind it was a large red button.

'This must be it,' shouted Robert excitedly as he jumped down from the chair. He was tall enough to reach the button, 'Are you ready?'

'Yes,' chorused Lucy & James. Robert pressed the button. There was a low whirring noise, and then, slowly, the central section of the bookcase began to slide backwards. Lucy realised that the noise she had heard earlier coming from the office must have been the sound of this secret doorway opening up.

There was no need for Robert and Lucy to ask whether James was in the room because they heard him gasp, 'Wow!' as he stepped inside. Robert noticed another button on the back of the bookcase. He pressed it, and the bookcase slowly slid back into place. Then Robert stepped back to take in the scene in front of them.

They had been worried that they would find Uncle Archie in some state of collapse inside, but there was no one else in the room. It was a room unlike any that they had seen before.

CHAPTER FOUR

'It's like a weird mix of science and history!' exclaimed James.

It was a long room. On the right was an enormous blackboard running the full length of the room. It was covered with writing; lists of numbers, dates, place names and historical periods ordered in precise, methodical columns. In front of the blackboard were five long mahogany desks. In contrast to the higgledy-piggledy nature of the desk in the first, dusty office, the books here were stacked in neat piles. On each desk were a notebook, a sharpened pencil and a box of chalk. On one of the desks was a laptop. Although switched off, it was connected by a network cable to a junction box on the wall, indicating access to the internet.

Down the left-hand side of the room were the machinery and equipment that had inspired James' comment about Science and History, for they looked both modern and antique. The materials certainly looked antique; there was an abundance of polished hardwoods: dark brown oak, deep red mahogany and the golden honeyed tones of beech. The historical nature was created by the fact that the predominant metal used was brass. Like everything else in the room, and again in contrast to the first office they had entered, the machines were spotlessly clean, gleaming and reflecting the light from the banks of strip lights suspended from the ceiling. There were chrome levers, brass buttons, white ceramic switches, but also (adding a scientific touch), rows of LED lights flashing on and off showing signs of activity.

Nestling in the centre of the room was the biggest computer that they had ever seen. The monitor wasn't big; it was no larger than the average laptop screen and built into the casing of the computer. It was the tower that was impressively large. Stretching right up to the ceiling, it resembled a stack of black briefcases, for it was made up of several components, each with a handle, stacked one upon the other. Some had buttons; some had dials very much like the security locks to be found on some suitcases. There were keypads and display screens, and again, LED lights twinkled, showing it was busy working away at something.

The far end of the room was completely separated by a floor to ceiling screen of thick smoked glass. In the centre was a close-fitting door, edged in chrome with a chrome handle, but they didn't need to go in to investigate because they could see it was completely empty. There were bare floorboards, nothing on the walls, just a window seat in front of the window that they had seen from the garden.

There were no curtains, just panelled wooden shutters, and no cushions on the window seat beneath it.

'It seems a lot of trouble to go to,' said Lucy looking up at the glass screen, 'In order to create a space with nothing in it!'

'So what now?' asked James.

'I think we have to go back upstairs,' said Robert, 'Let's wait and see if Uncle Archie comes back later tonight.'

'He wasn't there last night,' said James, 'I know because I looked in his room before I went out, and his bed hadn't been slept in.'

'That's funny,' said Lucy, 'Because when Robert and I looked in his room this morning, it looked as though his bed had been slept in.'

'I wonder if he comes in at breakfast time and messes the bed up to make Mrs Simpson think he has slept there all night,' said Robert.

'Maybe he is out all night,' said James. 'Maybe he's a vampire or a werewolf! Owwwwwww!'

'Shut up, James,' chorused Robert and Lucy.

***

The next morning the children were up early for breakfast. There was no sign of Uncle Archie; his bed still hadn't been slept in.

'We can't afford to let Mrs Simpson think that Archie has disappeared,' said James, 'She will ring up the school, and you two will have to go back, and they'd probably lock me up in hospital.'

'We'll do what we did last night,' said Robert, 'We'll pretend he's had his breakfast and gone back to work.'

'And we'll mess up his bed, so she thinks he's slept in it,' said Lucy.

'Why don't we tell Mrs Simpson that he's taking us out for a meal this evening, so she doesn't have to cook? That will give us at least 24 hours,' said James.

By the time Mrs Simpson arrived, all was prepared. There were four dirty plates and mugs piled in the sink. The cereal that Uncle Archie preferred had been left on the table, and his bed covers were in disarray. Lucy waited for Mrs Simpson whilst James and Robert went on ahead down to the museum. Lucy chose her words carefully; she didn't want to tell an actual lie.

'We're all going down to the museum this morning,' she said, 'The others have gone ahead. We've got some homework to do. I just wanted to let you know that we won't need a meal this evening as we are all eating out. Lucky us! It's nice to have a treat.'

'Oh, right you are then,' replied Mrs Simpson, 'I think I'll go and visit my sister if I don't have to get back. Are you alright with beans on toast for lunch?'

'Sounds delicious!' replied Lucy.

'Is James alright now? Haven't seen him for a while.'

'Nor have we,' thought Lucy, but she just smiled and nodded.

Soon all three of them were back down in the secret office. Nothing had changed since the previous evening. James had devised a way to stop Lucy and Robert bumping into him. He had stuffed a tennis ball into his pocket, and when he was standing or sitting in one place for a while, he would simply put it down on the floor beside him. After a short while, it would become visible and then Lucy and Robert knew to give him a wide berth. Sometimes he would bounce the ball as he walked, basketball style, and he found that when he had minimum contact with the ball, it didn't have time to become invisible. The problem was that basketball wasn't one of his strong points, and, invariably, the ball would end up bouncing away out of control.

'I think it will be a good idea if you stay in one place, so we know where you are,' said Robert.

'Where do we start?' asked James.

'I think we need to be organised.' replied Lucy, 'I'll see if there is anything useful on the laptop there. Robert, you look at the machines, and James, you take a look at the blackboard and also look at the notebooks. Let's give ourselves an hour and then get together and discuss what we have found.'

The hour seemed to go quickly. They realised they needed more time, so they gave themselves another hour and then another hour. There was so much to look at.

'We may as well discuss our findings while we eat our lunch,' said Robert. 'I'll function better once I have had my beans on toast!'

***

'I'll start,' said Robert. 'All the machines seem to be linked together; in fact, I think it is just one machine. There's a section with a large hinged lid made of rubber which clips onto a glass plate. It has pipes that feed into the back. It fooled me at first, but I think it's some kind of scanner. Perhaps it's for scanning objects rather than paper because I think the pipes are connected to a vacuum suction unit, which would hold an object in place. Then there's the large mainframe computer that probably controls everything. I wasn't going to touch that! After that, there's a section rather like a chest of drawers. The top has four sections, each containing rows of cut-out slots. It reminds me of a child's toy...one with different-shaped blocks of wood where you have to fit them through the right shaped holes. In the first section, the slots are filled with different-shaped blocks of wood, and each has a weird symbol carved on the top. I daren't move them, they must be important, but underneath are storage drawers with lots of spare blocks. From the last part of the machine, there are wires leading from the base of the cabinet and inserted into slots at the base of the giant glass screen. So all of this machinery is connected in some way to this glass, or perhaps to the space behind the glass.'

'Hmm!', said Lucy,' The symbols on these blocks, what do they look like?'

'I've got one here,' replied Robert, placing on the table a dark wooden block, with a silver base and a carved symbol on the top, 'Also, I made a copy of the symbols on the blocks in the machine.'

'Aha!', exclaimed Lucy, 'That explains it. I've seen that shape before. Remember, I was looking at the laptop, and first of all, I was asked for a six-letter password... Well *Archie* didn't work, but *museum* did, and then the next thing I was asked was what kind of keyboard *English* or *Runic*?'

'What's Runic?' asked James.

'You know, Runes! Ancient writing. Like in Lord of the Rings. The symbol on your block, Robert, is one of those Runes. There's more, though. There were only a few documents saved on that laptop; one was Shakespeare - a quote from Hamlet. At first, I thought it had been badly typed; it was as though the Shift key had been pressed at random intervals, so there was a mixture of capital letters and lower case letters. But then I thought that nothing else I've seen has been careless or random, and for some reason, I thought about the puzzle that Archie gave us. The code. And I realised that this was a code. Every time a letter appeared for the first time, it was capitalised, so what you end up with is the whole alphabet but in a different order. So I simply wrote out the alphabet, then wrote it out again underneath using the new order of letters and wrote a word out using this code, both with the English keyboard and with the Runic keyboard.'

'So what word did you write?' asked James, 'Was it your own name? That's what I would have done. My name is destined to be famous; I will have a star on the Hollywood pavement, it will be…'

'Oh shush,' interrupted Lucy, 'No, I did not. You will have seen the words written on the blackboard. Well, one was bigger than the others and was circled. Did you notice it?'

'Oh yes, of course,' said James. 'I noticed it straight away because it was the name of the town nearest to our school. Anchester.'

Lucy nodded and placed a printout from the laptop on the table.

'This is Anchester spelled out using the Runic code.'

Robert pulled out a piece of paper from his back pocket, unfolded it and spread it out below Lucy's paper. Making allowances for Robert's sketchy drawing, they could all see that they were the same.

'You said there were a few documents on the laptop?' asked Robert, 'What else was there?'

'Well, the piece from Hamlet gave the alphabet. Another document was a scan of an old train timetable like you might find in an antique shop, but random numbers had been circled with a pen. I am certain now that this will be another code to put the numbers nought to nine in a different order too. Funnily enough, the timetable was for trains from Anchester.'

'There aren't any trains that go to Anchester.' said

James.

'That's right,' said Lucy, 'but there used to be. The old station is now an Arts Centre.'

'Yes, and part of the school cross-country route uses the path where the rail tracks used to be,' said Robert. 'This is great progress. James, how about you? You were looking at the blackboard and at some of Archie's notebooks.'

'Well,' replied James, 'I do have some things to report, although I found looking at the books a bit difficult because when I picked them up, they disappeared, so I had to turn the pages with a pencil.'

Lucy and Robert glanced at each other. James seemed a bit flat. Lucy wondered if the difficulties of being invisible were getting him down. Robert wondered if it was a simple case of James not having anything to report to compare with their own findings, but neither said anything, and James continued.

'Well, I'll be brief. The blackboards are covered in writing, but some of the words have been circled. There are lots of place names, for instance, but, as you know, Anchester has been circled. There were lots of guns listed, such as *Mauser* and *Luger*, but *Walther PPK* was the one that was circled.'

'I wouldn't have known they were guns.'

'That's because you don't read the kind of books that I read, Lucy. The *Walther PPK* was the pistol that James Bond used. Actually, I read something about them in one of the notebooks. I didn't know that they date back to 1931 and that the German air force, the Luftwaffe, were issued with them in the Second World War. Anyway, you may have noticed that lines link some of the names on the boards and that this gun is linked to a list of dates which start from 1931. So there is a link, but from 1931 to 1939, they have been crossed out, so 1940 is the next one.'

'Well, that's good, James,' said Lucy 'We have three things, a place, a pistol and a date. We don't know the significance of them yet, but we can work on it. We're a good team. I don't know why you seem so disheartened?'

'Well, there is more. There's a blackboard with writing on it, maybe another code - I need your help Lucy, and there is this.' Whilst he had been talking, James had taken a piece of paper from his pocket and laid it on the table. At first, it was invisible, but as he finished speaking, the colour slowly flooded back.

'It fell out of one of the notebooks. I'll let you read it first.'

'Legend has it that the patient first experiences a general feeling of malaise: symptoms can include fatigue, depression, and nausea. As the condition develops, the pallor of the skin changes as the oxyhemoglobin levels reduce. This transcends levels associated with pallor mortis. In extreme cases, there are reports of patients disappearing from view entirely. There are no reports of patients surviving more than six months.'

'I didn't know whether I should show you at first.'

Lucy and Robert read the note, then sat in stunned silence for a few moments.

'Of course, you should have shown us. We are a team,' said Lucy; Robert nodded in agreement.

'Those are my symptoms,' said James, 'And Uncle Archie knew about it. Well, he knew that it might happen to one of us. I think he's been working on a cure, so we've got to find him, or else I've only got six months to live!'

'We are a team, remember,' said Lucy. 'So what we'll do is clear up here and get straight back down there. James, you and I will puzzle out what's written on that last blackboard, and Robert - you crack the code for the numbers from the timetable. It should be quite straightforward. Then look at the Runic blocks that are loaded into the machine. So we will be investigating this from both ends, from the beginnings on the blackboard to the end in the machine, and maybe somewhere in the middle will lie the answer to what it's all for, and where Uncle Archie might be.

***

It was a long day! The three of them had never studied so intently. Even Lucy, who was more accustomed to study, felt exhausted by the evening, so hard was she concentrating. They had heard the sound of the front door slamming shut as Mrs Simpson left to visit her sister. Before long, it was time for their evening meal.

'James and I will go out and buy something and bring it back here,' said Robert. 'We can't make a mess upstairs because Mrs Simpson thinks we're going out for a meal. What do you fancy? Fish and chips?'

James was now in high spirits, relieved because he had shared his awful secret. He and Robert went out to buy fish and chips, leaving Lucy to sit and puzzle.

'Be careful!' she said as she studied the writing on the blackboard. Right now, it didn't mean a lot to her, but she was determined that she would make sense of it. All too soon, the secret door swung open and in tumbled Robert and James, both laughing.

'Oh, that was funny,' said Robert, 'Do you know what he did? He kept making sounds – he started whistling, so I had to pretend to be whistling, then he started humming, which wasn't too bad, although I am sure I looked pretty daft.'

'You certainly did,' said James.

'But when we had to wait for a new batch of chips to be fried, he started tutting! I thought we were going to get thrown out of the shop, and then to cap it all, he started tap dancing!' continued Robert.

'Well, I don't think you passed the audition,' laughed James. 'Hollywood won't be calling you anytime soon.'

Lucy smiled; happy to see that her brothers' mood had lifted, she decided to wait until they had eaten their fish and chips before returning to the serious matter of working out the purpose of the strange machinery in Uncle Archie's office.

A short while later, Lucy stood before her brothers, pointing at the writing on the blackboard. Well, I figured out that the first part is about Uncle Archie. See - that's his birthday *18-05-1933*, I don't know what year he was born for sure, but I do know that his birthday is on May 18th, because it's written in my diary. You know how it's always me that remembers birthdays and buys the cards! You just sign them! Then there is *BORN LAT* and *BORN LON*.'

'Born late?' suggested Robert, 'and *LON* must mean London. We know Uncle Archie was born in London because he always puts on that hammy Cockney accent and re-enacts bits of '*Mary Poppins*.'

'Well, you are almost right', said Lucy, 'It is London, but *LAT* stands for latitude and *LON* for longitude. It's a map reference pinpointing exactly where Uncle Archie was born, and I think that's why Uncle Archie was asking us those questions about where we were born the other evening. Anyway, if you look at the rest of them, it starts to make sense,' continued Lucy, 'It's like a plane ticket, it says who it's for, then where from, and where to. It's from somewhere in Cambridge, and it's to somewhere in Anchester. Then there are some numbers headed by the titles *NOW-TIME, PAST-TIME* and *RETURN*. We need to check those map references; I'm sure we should be able to do it on the Internet.'

'I'll do that,' said Robert.

For the next hour, all was quiet. Lucy sat at one of the desks, notebook in hand, leafing through the diary. Robert sat in front of the computer, working out the longitude and latitude references. The only visible indication of James' presence was the sight of the Runic blocks from the drawers spiralling through the air to land in precise patterns on the floor. Only once was the silence broken when James went over to Robert to ask if he could work out the longitude and latitude of the house in Oxford where all three children were born. Once he had the answer, he returned to laying out the Runic blocks on the floor.

***

'I think we had better call it a day,' said Lucy 'Mrs Simpson might start getting concerned if we are too late back.'

'I don't think there's anything more I can do anyway,' said James, 'Look, using the code that's us on the floor' (James was actually pointing, which of course was a pointless thing for an invisible boy to do), but Robert and Lucy looked in the right direction anyway. There, neatly laid out on the floor, were three columns of key-code blocks.

'That's our personal information, laid out in the same way Uncle Archie's is. The only trouble is, I don't know what *NOW-TIME, PAST-TIME* and *RETURN* are.'

'Well, I'm going to take this diary back upstairs and continue reading it tonight. I'm sure the answer will be in here,' replied Lucy, 'Let's do exactly what we did this morning and, presuming Uncle Archie doesn't return, let's come down after breakfast.'

'I'll go in his room and mess up his bed and move some things around, so it looks like he's been home,' said Robert.

'Good idea,' said James, 'Only maybe I should do it – after all, I won't get seen in there by Mrs Simpson.'

'Are you sure you're alright?' said Lucy (the concern in her voice was quite noticeable), 'I am so worried about you.'

***

'It's incredible!' exclaimed Lucy excitedly the following day. 'I think I've figured most of it out.' Lucy had stayed up into the early hours of the morning reading the diary. Now the three of them were sitting in Uncle Archie's secret office. 'I'll come straight to the point: it's a time machine!'

'What?' exclaimed the two brothers in unison.

'Yes! Uncle Archie has been going back in time to look for something. It's all connected with us somehow. Uncle Archie has made lots of visits back to Anchester in the 1930s. He started in 1931 and, according to the Runic Blocks machine, right now he's stuck there in 1940.'

'Why is he there? What's he looking for?' asked James.

'Surely he is looking for a *Walther PPK*, ' interjected Robert.

'Yes, I think so,' replied Lucy. 'It doesn't actually say so in the diary, but that's my guess too. I don't know why he is looking for it.'

'But what about *NOW-TIME, PAST-TIME* and *RETURN?* asked James, aware that the blocks laid out on the floor were incomplete.

'I am fairly sure that *NOW-TIME* means how many hours he will be away in our time. So, the last time, he planned to be away for three hours. And the other one, *PAST-TIME*, means how many hours he has got when he gets there.'

'Well, we had better go and find him,' said Robert jumping up, 'He may need our help, and James certainly needs his help.'

'Yes, but not so fast,' replied Lucy, 'Look, I can't be certain about all of this; I've been thinking about this all night. I think we ought to test drive it. We don't want to get stuck way back in the past if we do something wrong. I think we ought to set the machine up to go back just a few days. Then if it all goes wrong, and we can't get back, we'll only have a few days to wait to get back to now. We can't set the machine to take us back to Anchester now or, say, yesterday because what if someone sees us? We're supposed to be on holiday. I think the best day to go back to would be the day our holiday started when we were waiting to come here.'

'So do we become ourselves, sitting in the reception room, or will there be two of me?' asked Robert.

'I really don't know,' said Lucy 'We will just have to be very, very careful.'

'Come on,' said Robert 'No time like the present.'

'Was that a joke?' asked James

'No, I mean, let's get the machine set up and go straight away.'

'What do we do with Uncle Archie's settings?' asked James.

'I think we should leave them. There are three more columns where we can put our key-code blocks,' replied Lucy.

'I just can't believe it,' said James, 'A time machine! Then again, I would never have believed that I could become invisible!'

CHAPTER FIVE

Archie Baxter was finding it difficult to get comfortable on the thin, narrow mattress. He turned over and faced the cell wall and wondered what was to become of himself. The painted brick walls were a particularly unpleasant shade of green with condensation streaming down and lying in pools on the concrete floor. Despite it being a Spring morning, the air was cold and damp. Archie recognised that he had been foolish. He had underestimated the level of trepidation and mistrust in 1940s wartime England. He thought he had come across as friendly and chatty when he enquired if there were any captured Germans prisoners nearby, but someone must have reported him. He remembered now that it was only back in February that the government had launched a poster campaign: 'Careless Talk Costs Lives', and now, instead of finding a German prisoner who might have hidden a *Walther PPK* somewhere, he himself was the prisoner. He had very little idea of just how he might get back to the 21st Century.

Further along the corridor, Captain Bracewaite strolled into the Duty Sergeant's office.

'Sir,' barked out the sergeant, jumping up from his chair and saluting.

'Good morning Sarge. At ease. So, fill me in about our new arrival. What do we know about him?'

'Not very much, sir. He was spotted hanging around the railway station asking questions. Something about him, sir, the way he speaks, something different. I mean, he sounds English, but sometimes he says things in a funny way. And he ain't got no proper papers with him. Says his name is Archibald Baxter and that he's from Cambridge. And that's all he's saying, sir. I reckon he's a German spy.'

'Hmm! Dashed inconvenient if you ask me,' replied Captain Bracewaite. 'I'd better get in touch with HQ. They might want to send a chap down from London. There's no point in me going in there and asking a load of questions right now. We'll let him stew a while. Right, that's all for now; keep up the good work.'

***

Back in Cambridge, the three Baxter children were all prepared. They had set out the Runic blocks on the machine using the personal information that Robert and James had compiled. The date differed from Uncle Archie's column: they set the date to be the day they had left school. They were not entirely sure about what to set for *RETURN*.

'Uncle Archie mentions making changes to the *NOW-TIME* and *PAST-TIME* settings in his diary.' said Lucy.

'That's why I think *NOW-TIME* is how long we are going to be away; it's nearly 10 o'clock now so I think two hours should be OK. We won't be missed. As for how much time we need when we get there, well, how about three hours? Then for *RETURN*, I've no idea, so maybe we'd better leave that the same.'

'OK,' said Robert, 'Then we're all set. There's a button on the Runic Block machine, closest to the glass screen, that says *START*. I'm rather hoping that all we have to do is press it. I don't know how much time we have to get inside, so why don't you two go and sit on the seat ready? Lucy, you sit in the middle, and James, you sit on the right, so I don't end up sitting on your lap.'

With Lucy and James in place, Robert's finger hovered over the *'START'* button. He breathed in deeply, jabbed down hard on the button, then dashed behind the glass screen and sat down on the window seat. They noticed a change immediately; the lights in the room dimmed, the computer in the centre of the machinery started to hum, and a light on the Runic Block machine turned first red, then amber. Then… nothing! Lucy, despite her organised and confident demeanour, was feeling very nervous. She stretched out her hands, feeling first for James' hand on one side, and then she took hold of Robert's hand on the other side, squeezing hard for comfort. This action seemed to be what the machine required. Perhaps it was used to dealing with just one person, Uncle Archie, and it needed the three children to be physically connected. The amber light turned green, and the three children felt a sensation similar to one that they had experienced on a fairground ride. It was as though they were on a big dipper, plunging first down into blackness, then a gradual climb up into light. Lucy had screamed at first, and all three had involuntarily screwed their eyes shut but, as they became aware that they had stopped moving and that the room was light and warm, they opened them to find that they were no longer in Cambridge.

***

Lucy recognised where they were first.

'It's the Arts Centre,' she whispered. They were sitting in the window of what was once the waiting room for the Anchester Railway station but was now a gallery space. Like many small provincial railway stations, it had been closed by the government back in the 1960s when Dr Beeching had attempted to modernise the railway system. The track had been taken up and was now a grassed public footpath, and the building, after lying dormant for many years, had benefited from a grant to develop it into a community Arts Centre. An architect had unified the railway buildings into one, introducing glass and steel, so that what was once an outside platform was now a light and airy gallery space, but parts of the original building, including the room that the children were in, had been restored to reflect their former use. The fireplace, although not in working order, had been restored. The walls were hung with framed railway posters, and the room was lined with an assortment of hard wooden chairs, all antique and all looking very uncomfortable!

'I can hardly believe it!' breathed Lucy.

James had hoped that, as he was going back in time, he would no longer be invisible, but he was disappointed.

'What now?' he asked.

'Well, we've proved that Uncle Archie's machine can transport us,' said Lucy, 'And we'll be able to check the date by looking at a newspaper, but I am curious to know whether we've replaced our normal selves, or whether we've duplicated ourselves, and the only way we can do that is by catching a bus back to school.'

'Have you got any money?' asked Robert. 'I haven't.'

He looked down at himself – he was wearing different clothes from the ones he had worn back in Cambridge. Then, he had been wearing casual but sporty clothes. Now he was wearing his school sports clothes; tracksuit bottoms, a sweatshirt, and running shoes.

'Actually, I don't think I had any money with me when we set off.'

'No, I haven't brought any money,' said James.

Lucy also was wearing different clothes; she now had her school uniform on, but she also had her bag. She checked inside to find that she still had her purse with a small amount of money in it.

'I've enough for the day,' she said breezily. 'After all, we've only come for three hours. Let's get going. We should just have time to catch the 10.30 bus from the marketplace.

The journey to school was pretty uneventful. There weren't many people on the bus, so James had no problem finding himself a seat. As the bus drew away, Robert and Lucy found their way down the aisle, and they noticed that James's tennis ball had materialised on a seat near the back of the bus. Robert sat down next to it to prevent any unsuspecting passenger sitting on James. Although, as the crow flies, it was only three miles from the Arts Centre to the school, the bus meandered through the neighbouring villages, and it was thirty minutes before the Baxters leapt off the bus, just around the corner from the school gates.

'I'll go and see if the coast is clear,' whispered James. 'Wait here.' A moment later, he was back.

'There is no one in sight at the gates,' he said, 'Why

don't we sneak around the back of the Quad onto the playing field where no one will see us.

Hidden behind a rose bush, at the edge of the playing field, they continued their conversation.

'It's obvious!' exclaimed James, 'It has to be me. No one can see me, so I have to be the one who goes to reception. We need to know how all this works. Do we exist here right now, behind this bush, as well as in the reception room?'

'Well, be careful,' said Lucy. 'Also, I've just realised that we only have fifteen minutes before we get the bus back. They only come once an hour, and if we wait for the one after, we'll be too late to get back to the Arts Centre.'

'Don't worry,' said James reassuringly. I won't be long,' and he ran off in the direction of the Reception Room.

'I can't believe that we have come back to school in our holidays!' whispered Robert.

'I know,' replied Lucy, 'My mood keeps swinging from worry about James's condition and because Uncle Archie has disappeared, through to utter amazement and excitement that we've travelled through time and space.'

'By the way, did you notice that man reading a newspaper on the bus?' said Robert, 'It was from the day we left; I recognised the headlines, so unless he was reading an old paper, which I doubt, then it confirms the fact that we have travelled back in time.'

'Oh James, hurry up!' exclaimed Lucy.

James was having a decidedly odd experience. The windows to the reception room were too high to look through from the outside, so he decided to go into the room. He carefully turned the handle and let the door swing open, as though the wind were blowing it, skipped inside, then gently pushed it closed again. He scanned the room. The receptionist had looked up from her computer when the door opened but was now engrossed again. In the seats near the window was the familiar sight of his brother and sister, but what unnerved James was seeing himself sitting across the room. He had seen himself on video before (the school plays were always filmed), but that didn't prepare him for the actual shock of seeing himself in three dimensions. He waited, breathing silently and standing still, wondering if the James looking bored and rather poorly, would be able to sense the fact that he was standing there, but no, there was no response.

'Really, why should there be?' James thought, 'Because surely I would have remembered it.' There was not even an unconscious flicker of movement in recognition of the fact that he was face-to-face with his own self, even if it was an invisible version of himself.

James quietly tiptoed over to where Lucy was sitting. He noticed the two puzzle books sticking out of her bag. He reached over and held one of them. Gradually it faded from view, and, once it was invisible, he pulled it out of the bag and stuffed it into his pocket. Next, James was curious about what Miss Rodgers, the receptionist, was doing on the computer. Instead of school-related work, James saw the screen was filled with rows of handbags. She looked around for a moment to check on the Baxters. She, too, wished that whoever was supposed to be collecting them would arrive; their presence was distracting her from her online shopping! Robert couldn't resist; whilst her head was turned, he reached over to her computer and closed her web page down. When she looked back, she could barely contain her annoyance at losing her page of handbags. So focused on the screen was she that she didn't notice the door gently open as James slipped back outside.

Meanwhile, Robert had been getting impatient and couldn't resist standing up from behind the rose bush to see what could be keeping James. Immediately he regretted it because across the field boomed the voice of one of his teachers.

'Baxter!' It was Mr Foster, the sports teacher, 'Baxter, over here!'

'Yes sir,' called Robert and ran over to where Mr Foster was standing. For a sports teacher, Mr Foster was a very un-athletic specimen. He was overweight, out of condition, and never ran if he could walk, and never stood if he could sit.

'I thought you were going home for Easter,' he said.

'I am, sir, soon.'

'Well, you are just the chap I need. I seem to have left a notebook on the other side of the field, by the bench. Be a good chap and go and fetch it, bring it up to the staff room.'

'B'but I'm going home,' stuttered Robert.

'Well, what time are you going?' interrupted Mr Foster. Robert had to think quickly; he couldn't afford to say anything that would deviate from what actually happened.

'In about twenty-five minutes, sir.'

'Well, you have plenty of time, a fast runner like you. Are you all packed and bags in reception?'

'Yes, sir.'

Robert noticed that, behind Mr Foster's back, a tennis ball had materialised on the ground. It then danced about in the air before slowly becoming invisible. Robert realised that James was standing close by, listening to the conversation.

'Look, tell you what,' said Mr Foster, 'I'll drop into reception and let Miss Rodgers know where you are.'

'No!' blurted out Robert. He realised that that would be disastrous because his teacher might then encounter another Robert Baxter who would be totally unaware of the situation. 'I mean, no, there's no need. I've plenty of time. I'll go and get the notebook and bring it up to you. Really, it's alright, sir.'

'Fine,' said Mr Foster, turning on his heels and feeling quite pleased with himself in managing to avoid walking right across the field again.

'James, are you there,' whispered Robert.

'Yes, I'm still here,' came the reply, 'And I'm in reception too, we all are!'

'Look, you and Lucy go to the bus stop,' said Robert. 'If I miss the bus I'll get to the Arts Centre somehow. Don't wait for me.' Without waiting for a reply, Robert turned and ran off in the direction of the bench on the far side of the sports field to look for Mr Foster's notebook. Unfortunately, it wasn't there.'

'Oh no!' panted Robert, 'Now what?' Robert had no idea where else Mr Foster had been, so he was forced to zigzag his way back across the field, scanning the ground for signs of the lost notebook. Finally, he arrived back at the entrance to the school. He still hadn't found it. He took the steps up to the staff room two at a time. On his way, he met two of his classmates.

'Hello, Robert. Thought you were going home today. Changed your mind?'

'I'm still going,' panted Robert, pausing for a moment, 'I've just got to go and see Mr Foster,' and, without prolonging the conversation, he bounded along the corridor and knocked on the staff room door. Mr Foster himself opened it.

'Ah, there you are!' said Mr Foster before Robert had

time to speak, 'Surprised it took you so long because it wasn't there, was it?' Robert shook his head.

'Sorry young man,' continued Mr Foster, holding up a maroon notebook, 'It was in my jacket pocket all along. Well, you'd better run along; you don't want to miss your lift home, do you?' Mr Foster smiled and shut the door. Robert looked upwards in exasperation, then turned and ran back down the corridor to try and catch the bus.

A few minutes later, Robert was standing in front of an empty bus stop; he must have missed it. Not only that, he realised that Lucy had all the money.

'Oh no! Now what?'

***

Archie Baxter slowly opened his eyes. He was lying on his bed, facing the wall of his prison cell.

'I must have dropped off,' he thought. 'I wonder what time it is?' Something was different. Apart from the fact that he felt unusually drowsy, there were other differences. As he lay there without moving, he closed his eyes and started to list the differences.

'I definitely am warmer than I have been for a while,' he thought, 'And this bed cover doesn't feel as rough. Also, the clothes I am wearing seem to fit better.' Then something else slowly dawned on him. Very faintly, he could hear music coming from another cell. Whilst he could not make out what it was, there was something about the drumbeat and the rhythm of the music that made it unlike any music that came from wartime Britain. He opened his eyes again, and another thing struck him, something he should have noticed the first time he opened his eyes. The walls were white and had been plastered, not bricks painted green. He sat up abruptly, hitting his head as he did so. Another difference; he was now in a bunk bed.

'Oy!' came a threatening voice from above. 'I'm trying to get some rest here, pal!' Archie surveyed the rest of the room. There was no doubt about it; he was in a modern prison cell, and he couldn't think how he got there.

***

Meanwhile, Pete Briggs, one of the prison officers, was at home tucking into burger and chips and, between mouthfuls, was complaining to his wife, Sharon.

'I tell you, it's a blooming shambles! Left-hand doesn't know what the right one is doing. There's this one downstairs right, he's just been transferred in from somewhere, but there's no paperwork! Don't know what he's in for, don't know his name even. Looks like they are going to have to interview him and ask him! I mean, how does that make us look! We are supposed to bang people up, not lose them in the system! Blooming shambles!'

'Oh, it's a shame,' commiserated his wife.

'Watchoo talkin about! Shame! Shame for who? Shame for us, more like. I mean, how do we know how to treat him? Some people get transferred because they've been somewhere tougher but have been on best behaviour, and it's a reward like. But it might be the other way round. He might have been in some soft prison, and he might be a real hard nut, right? Blooming shambles!'

***

Robert was running. He had realised that was the only way that he could get to the Arts Centre in time. He had two advantages that gave him hope. Firstly, running was something he felt born to do. He had been fairly modest about his athletic prowess when it was a topic of conversation with Uncle Archie. He had been too modest to mention that he was the current holder of the Stephen Archway Cup, a trophy for cross-country running awarded in memory of one of the School Old Boys, a war hero. Secondly, whereas the bus zigzagged its way to the Market Place through neighbouring villages, he could take the most direct route to the Arts Centre: the railway track itself. Most of the track was a cultivated nature trail, and much of it was very familiar to him because the school cross-country route used part of it before circling back towards the school. It would be tight, and he was not confident that he could get there in time, but he had to try.

As Robert ran, he was reminded about the last time he had run this route. It hadn't been a serious race, just a regular sports lesson. Robert and a few others were in a pack of runners well ahead of the others. The point where the school cross-country route left the old railway path was just before a short tunnel; the route then headed along footpaths through farmland before turning back in the direction of the school. For the schoolboys, the tunnel had a name; it was reputed to be haunted, and the schoolchildren always referred to it as 'Old Growler's' tunnel. Whilst the tunnel was structurally safe, very few people passed through it. Boys from the school were scared of the 'ghost', and walkers coming from the town centre rarely ventured that far: it was dark and damp in there. The boys running the race were daring each other to run through the tunnel and back, and Robert and his friend Stephen took on the dare. As Robert ran through the tunnel, he noticed out of the corner of his eye that there was a doorway leading to a room built into the side of the tunnel. Then, his heart froze as he heard a muttering and grumbling noise slowly build to a full-throated roar. He looked towards Stephen and, although it was too dark to see him, he sensed his fear. Logic told the two boys that it was probably a vagrant, sleeping rough down there, annoyed at being disturbed, but that logic wasn't enough to persuade them to run back through the tunnel to continue the race, so instead, they chose to climb up the side of the bank and run over the fields at the top of the tunnel: a much longer route. By the time they had reached the school, their courage had returned. The story had been somewhat exaggerated and would be added to the school folklore about the existence of 'Old Growler.'

Robert paused as he reached the tunnel once more. Whilst he knew that the path would take him all the way to the old railway station (now the Arts Centre), he had never gone further than the tunnel and therefore did not know how far he still had to run. He did not think he could afford the time to climb all the way over the top, so he knew that he would have to summon up enough courage to go through the tunnel and risk an encounter with 'Old Growler'. Instead of running headlong into danger, this time, he decided to creep silently and tentatively down the tunnel, fully prepared to sprint either back down the way he had come or ahead towards the station should it become necessary. All was quiet. He reached the position of the doorway and, this time, was able to focus through the gloom. He saw that there was a small room, its walls lined in brick. The door was open and hanging half off. He could make out signs that someone had been living there, perhaps they still were, for there were bottles, cans and packaging from fast food strewn about on the floor, and a bundle of something, perhaps a sleeping bag, lying on a bench seat that ran the length of the room. For now, the room was empty, no danger. Robert switched his mind back to the matter in hand. He had to get to the Arts Centre and meet up with Lucy and James in time to be in position to journey forwards to their rightful place in the future. Robert started to run once more.

***

For Lucy and James, the journey to the Arts Centre had been much quicker and less strenuous than it was proving to be for Robert. They now had half an hour to spare before the time when they had to be sitting on the window seat in the old waiting room in order to carry on through time and space and end up in Cambridge. Lucy thought it best if they spent that time in the Arts Centre, she had noticed that a new exhibition was being set up as they arrived.

'Homecoming,' she read from the poster outside, 'Illustrious artist Mary Cairns returns to Anchester for a retrospective exhibition.' She pushed on the door and held it open for a moment so that James could slip in unnoticed.

'We close in 20 minutes, you know,' came an imperious voice from within the gallery. 'We are closing early because Mary Cairns is giving a talk about her work to invited guests.' By the tone of her voice, Lucy suspected that the speaker did not welcome schoolchildren into the gallery, especially so near to closing time.

'Oh, that's okay,' replied Lucy compliantly, 'I'll just have a quick look around.' Lucy felt far from okay though, not only did she need an extra ten minutes, but she also wasn't sure if Robert was going to arrive.

'Don't worry, leave her to me,' whispered James into her ear.

Lucy decided to distract herself from her worries by looking at the exhibition. The paintings were all landscapes. The first ones she came to were large and bright with splashy brushstrokes. They featured a patchwork of fields and trees, all depicted with areas of pattern; spots, stripes and zigzags. The label at the side of each picture gave the date and name of the painting. They were named after the English counties that they were painted in. Lucy moved to the next room. Here the style was quite different. The paintings were smaller; the brush strokes were smoother, and they had an almost photographic appearance. As she read the labels, Lucy realised that these paintings were all produced in America. She also realised that she was probably walking around the exhibition in the wrong direction because they were older than the first paintings she had looked at. There was another lady in the room. She looked quite old and was so small that she was about the same size as Lucy. She looked up and smiled at Lucy.

'I like this exhibition' said Lucy. 'It's a pity it closes soon. I'll have to come back. Did you know that these were all painted in America, and in that other room, they were all painted in this country? – I don't know what's in the far room yet.'

'Yes, my dear,' replied the lady, 'I painted them. I'm Mary Cairns. The other room has some very early paintings that I produced at Art School when I moved away from home to live in New York. It's even got a few drawings that I did as a child when I lived briefly in this area. That's how it all started, really. But, goodness me! Look at the time. I'm giving a talk in an hour, so I had better go and look at my notes. It was very nice to talk to you, Lucy. Why don't you have this exhibition catalogue? Normally the gallery sells them, but I am giving you my copy.'

'It was very nice to meet you too.' replied Lucy, as Mary Cairns rushed out of the room, and then, as she stuffed the catalogue into her bag, she wondered, 'That's strange, how did she know my name?'

Meanwhile, James was shadowing the lady who had warned them that the gallery was shutting early. Miss Rook was fussing around, trying to get everything ready for Mary Cairns' talk. She didn't really need to shut early. The gallery was ready, the chairs arranged in rows. Refreshments had been laid out on the table, biscuits on plates, cups and saucers waiting to be filled with tea or coffee, and wine glasses arranged in neat lines. The catering staff would be returning just before the talk began.

Robert still hadn't arrived. It was now ten minutes away from the time that they should return to the future. Miss Rook glanced at her watch.

'Oh, she really has to go,' she muttered to herself and turned to walk in the direction of the room where Lucy was. James silently raced in the opposite direction to the large glass window that looked out on the site of the old railway line, now replaced by an ornamental flower garden. He rapped hard on the window, which halted Miss Rook in her tracks. Puzzled, she walked over to see where the noise was coming from. She peered in all directions through the window but could see no one there. James, standing quite close, held his breath. Turning, Miss Rook walked in the direction of Lucy and, once again, James knocked on the window, bringing her back to the glass. James' delaying tactics even worked a third time, but the fourth time he did it, even though she stopped and turned, Miss Rook shook her head and turned to thread her way between the chairs and the refreshment table to seek out Lucy. James rushed forwards. Just as Miss Rook passed a basket perched near the edge of the table containing packets of sugar, James reached out and tipped it over, scattering the contents on the floor.

'Oh botheration!' exclaimed Miss Rook, presuming that her clothing must have caught it, and she dropped to her hands and knees to gather the packets up. Just then,

Robert burst through the door.

'We are closing!' shouted Miss Rook from below the table.

'I've just come for my sister,' panted Robert, flushed from the exertions of his run.

'Well. find her and go!'

Robert felt James's hand clutch his arm.

'This way,' he whispered.

After looking at Mary's schoolgirl crayon drawings of an Oxfordshire farm nearby, Lucy had left the gallery and was already anxiously sitting in the window seat in the old waiting room. With only thirty seconds to go, James and Robert sat down beside her, and Lucy held on tightly to their hands. They heard Miss Rook's footsteps approaching, but they were no longer there when she marched into the room.

'I thought I made myself clear...' She stopped. The room was empty. The three Baxter children were already back in Cambridge!

***

Archie Baxter was puzzled. He was still in the same prison cell, but when he had gone to bed, he had been on the bottom bunk bed, with a rather threatening Liverpudlian in the bunk above his head. Now he opened his eyes to find that he was on the top bunk. He peered below. The bottom bunk was empty. It clearly hadn't been slept in. There was a jangle of keys; the door swung open, and in walked Pete Briggs, the prison officer.

'Oy, sleeping beauty!' he barked. The Governor wants to see you in half an hour. Have you forgotten, I told you yesterday?'

'I don't remember that,' replied Archie, 'What for? What day is it?'

75

'Give me strength!' sighed Pete, 'I don't know why he wants to see you do I? And it's Tuesday.'

'Are you sure?' replied Archie, remembering something from his previous day in the cell, 'There was a football match on yesterday, England versus Portugal; it was a Saturday.'

'England versus Portugal!' That was a couple of weeks ago.' Then Pete's mood darkened, 'Listen, grandpa, if you keep messing me around, I could make life very difficult for you. Now get yourself ready – the Governor doesn't like to be kept waiting.'

Archie pondered for a moment before tidying himself up for his appointment with the Governor.

'First I was in 1940, then somehow I was dragged back into this century, and then I jumped forward a couple of weeks. Either the 'Machine' back in Cambridge is malfunctioning, or someone else is using it!'

CHAPTER SIX

Back in Cambridge, the 'Machine' was being prepared to be used again. After a good night's sleep, the Baxter children were losing no time in setting off to search for Archie, not realising that at that very moment, he was in a prison just a few hours' car ride away, not decades away.

'This time, we'll be better prepared,' said Lucy, with a rueful glance at Robert, 'With money, for instance!' Robert pulled a face, but Lucy didn't notice, as she was busy checking the contents of her bag. She had scissors, sewing needles and thread, sticky tape, ballpoint pens, a notebook, a sketchbook and a pack of different coloured felt-tip pens.

'Right,' said James, 'I'll just go over the settings once more. We are travelling back in time to 1940, going to Anchester station again. We'll stay for the whole day, returning from there at eight o'clock in the evening, but when we arrive back here, we'll only have been missing for an hour. If the worst happens and we get held up, we can come back at twelve midnight.'

'This time, we won't have to worry about meeting anyone we know,' said Robert.

'You can worry about the fact that there will be a war on!' Lucy pointed out.

'Oh, it'll be alright,' came James's voice from the direction of the 'Machine'. 'After all, we know England wasn't invaded, and we're only there for a few hours, and we know where we are going to. What can go wrong? Come on, let's get on with it.'

Once more, the children held hands and felt like they were plunging into an abyss. Gradually, the swoop down through time came to a halt, light filtered through the darkness, and once again, they found themselves sitting in the window seat at Anchester station. Only this time, it looked very different. The walls were painted a sludgy green, and the door and the window frame were painted chocolate brown, a contrast to the white walls and stripped pine woodwork that were to feature when it became a 21st century Arts Centre. The room wasn't the only thing that was different. Robert and Lucy looked at each other and burst out laughing. It hadn't occurred to them that they would be wearing 1940s clothing! Lucy was wearing a checked pinafore dress, woven in a rather itchy wool. She had on a grey knitted cardigan, and she was carrying a grey raincoat. Robert, too was mostly dressed in grey. He was used to wearing sports shorts, but the shorts he found himself wearing now were distinctly un-fashionable, as were the long grey socks!

'What's that?' asked Lucy, pointing to a label held by a

safety pin to his sleeveless patterned pullover. 'Why, it's got your name written on it!'

'You've got one too,' said James. 'I can feel that there's one pinned to me as well, and I think I've got a case like yours. I can feel it between my feet.' Lucy and Robert looked down and noticed that they each had a small, battered brown suitcase. The cases were shiny, like leather, but they could see where the corners were scuffed that they were actually made of cardboard.

Then, suddenly, they were not alone. There was a hoot from a steam train outside, and at the same time, the door burst open and in tumbled four more children who dodged around the waiting room chairs, laughing and shouting as they tried to catch each other. Their impromptu game of tag was brought to a halt when a large figure loomed in the doorway.

'Come out of there this instant!' she boomed. 'How dare you, you little scoundrels.' Whilst they could not see her face, as she was silhouetted in the doorway, the children could tell that she was a woman of authority. She wore a long coat, a hat and was carrying a notebook in one hand and a fountain pen in the other. The boys stopped dead in their tracks and sheepishly trudged out of the room. The woman looked towards Lucy and Robert, still sitting in the window seat and looking very stunned.

'Are you deaf?' she yelled.

'N,no,' stuttered Lucy.

'I said, 'come out of there.' Don't you know there's a war on? Now come and join the others.'

James clung on tight to Lucy's arm as they left the waiting room and ventured onto the platform. It was as much for his own reassurance as for Lucy's comfort, as they had not expected to be so much the centre of attention. A train was still waiting, steam curling onto the platform. It gave another short, impatient blast of its whistle. Men in uniforms, carrying large kitbags, were clambering onto the train. Others were leaning out of the windows, shouting and joking, whilst wives, sweethearts and mothers stood on the platform clutching handkerchiefs, holding back tears and smiling and nodding in encouragement.

For a moment, the children wondered if they were going to be forced to get on the train and be taken far away from Anchester, but instead, they followed the other boys to walk past the ticket office and out onto the pavement outside. In front of an unfamiliar small red-bricked house, they saw a straggly line of thirty or forty children, all carrying small cases and all with labels pinned to their clothing.

'Now get back in line,' they were told. They joined the end, behind the four boys who had been playing tag and who were still attempting to play the game without leaving their place in the queue.

'Listen to me!' shouted the lady with the notebook and fountain pen. She had a voice that demanded to be listened to! 'You will follow me; we will walk in single file to the Corn Exchange, and no wandering off!'

She marched to the front of the queue. Two other ladies joined the line at the end, behind Robert Lucy and James, and they set off, walking through the streets of Anchester. The children realised that, at the moment, there was clearly no escape. They were not in control of their own destiny.

It was a disturbing experience. The town, whilst familiar in some respects, was also different from the Anchester they knew. There was the red-brick house adjacent to the station, which they had never seen before, but also the shops looked quite different too. Gone were the large windows, colourful displays of clothes, interspersed with fast food shops. Instead, windows were smaller, often shuttered. There was painted wood instead of chrome. There were one or two shops with clothes in the windows, but there were many more shops selling food than they remembered; butchers, bakers, greengrocers and fishmongers. Many of the buildings looked familiar, but the children were conscious that there were changes (buildings missing) without being able to pinpoint exactly what was different.

As the crocodile passed, the shopkeepers came to their doorways and stared, as did the early morning shoppers. For the three children, it was disturbing in a different way, because they had recently watched a wartime movie, set in Poland, and they realised that they alone in the queue knew that similar scenarios were being re-enacted throughout Germany, only the children were all Jewish, and their fate was to be much more uncertain.

Finally, they arrived at an imposing building in the main town square. 'I don't remember seeing this building before', whispered Lucy, as they climbed the steps to a large open doorway. Eventually, the whole group was assembled in a big room. It had a patterned, tiled floor in terracotta, blue, and white. The walls were lined with portraits of men wearing waistcoats and hats and sporting an array of beards and moustaches. The children fidgeted, some whispered to each other, a few of the younger children were sobbing, but mostly they were silent. The lady from the front of the queue now stood before them on a podium.

'My name is Miss Spencer, and I am the Billeting Officer for Anchester and the surrounding districts. I have therefore been given the task of finding homes for you because the Government thinks it is not safe for you to remain in London. In a moment, the good people of the town will enter, and you will be allocated new homes. First of all, though, I will check your names against my list.'

By the time Miss Spencer reached Lucy and Robert, she was not in a good mood.

'Name?' she asked.

'Lucy Baxter.'

'And you?' she asked, looking at Robert.

'Robert Baxter'. Behind Robert, with his hands gently gripping both his brother and sister, James held his breath.

'I might have known it would be you!' exploded Miss Spencer. 'You are the two who sneaked into the waiting room. You two are not on my list. Now I am going to have to re-jig everything.' With that, she stormed off to consult with her two colleagues.

***

Thirty minutes later, the three children were enduring a cold and bumpy ride sitting in an open trailer being pulled by a small, rusty, red tractor. The tractor itself was also open to the elements, with just the one seat, astride which sat Joe Sinclair. Joe was a worried man; his wife Martha was what some people would describe as 'A strong woman.' He preferred the word 'bossy' but wouldn't dare say it to her face! The Sinclairs had been told they had no choice and they had to take an evacuee, so she had sent him out to pick a strong-looking girl; Martha wanted some more help with the housework. Joe looked over his shoulder to see the two children clinging onto the sides of the trailer. He could not see the third, of course, James, who was squashed in beside his sister. When finally the tractor stopped outside Highfield Farm, Martha's reaction was just as Joe had feared.

'Two? Have you taken leave of your senses? How are we going to feed two extra mouths?'

'I, I wasn't given a choice,' stuttered Joe, 'they told me I had to take both of them. They are brother and sister.'

'Well, they had better come in and get warm, but the boy is going to have to sleep in the barn, so you had better get it ready. The box room isn't big enough for two, and I'm not having strangers sleeping in our Billy's room.'

Joe went to the back of the trailer and unhooked the tailgate, making it easier for the children to jump down.

So, what's your names then?' asked Martha.

'I'm Lucy, Lucy Baxter.'

'And I'm Robert Baxter.'

'Well, you had better come in; there's a fire lit inside. I'll put the kettle on.'

Lucy and Robert followed Martha through a door so tiny that Robert had to stoop to enter the dark interior beyond. Lucy and Robert paused and bent down to untie the laces on their shoes, as taking their shoes off was something they would normally do when visiting someone's home. Martha glanced behind her to check they had shut the door and noticed them struggling to untie the knots.

'What on earth are you doing?' she asked.

'Just taking off my shoes,' replied Lucy sheepishly, at the same time noticing the muddy footprints on the red quarry-tiled floor.

'Is that what they do in London?' asked Martha incredulously. 'Where do you think you are? Buckingham Palace? We'll have none of that here, I for one, am not darning your socks when they wear out.'

Lucy and Robert looked around the room, rather thankful they didn't have to walk on the cold tiled floor just in their socks. They were standing in a small kitchen. In front of the window was a deep white ceramic sink; opposite it was a black cast iron kitchen range. Lucy was familiar with Aga range cookers, with their shiny steel covers over their hot plates. One of her friends had a cream one in their kitchen, and another friend had a blue one, but this was altogether a smaller and more basic design. She could see the flicker of light coming from the flames that heated the hot plate. Lucy presumed her friends' cookers ran on gas, but this one was clearly burning coal because there was a galvanised steel bucket filled with coal by the side of it. Robert noticed only the kettle that was boiling merrily on top of it. Ordinarily, he rarely drank tea, preferring to drink cola or lemonade but, apart from the fact that he sensed that asking for a soft drink might not be the best of ideas, he also was looking forward to a hot drink to warm himself up from the cold ride in the trailer.

'You can go through into the parlour,' said Martha, gesturing towards the door behind her. 'I've lit the fire - don't normally at this time of year, except Sunday sometimes. We keeps warm by the stove, but I knows it's a cold ride on that trailer cos I've done it myself!'

Lucy and Robert trooped through, followed by James, who was trying his best not to make a noise and not trip over Lucy's feet whilst holding on to her arm to reassure her that he was still there. It was another small and dark room. There was an oil lamp perched on a table next to a wooden rocking chair, but it was not lit. There was a comforting warm glow from the fire that burned in a modest black iron fireplace. On the mantelpiece leant a frame with a black and white photograph of two very ancient-looking people standing stiffly in front of the same farmhouse that they were in. Next to it was a wooden clock with the loudest tick that the children had ever heard. Just then, it chimed once; it was now one o'clock. There wasn't much in the way of comfortable seating in the room. Apart from the rocking chair, there were just two rather lumpy armchairs with wooden arms and cracked brown leather seats. Lucy chose one of the armchairs, and James perched on its arm. Robert hovered near the fire, he sensed that the rocking chair was probably Joe's usual place to sit, but he still felt chilled by their journey in the back of the trailer. The clatter of cups from the kitchen could be heard as Martha prepared a pot of tea.

'What are we going to do?' whispered James. 'When do we have to get back?'

'I don't know,' replied Lucy, 'I've no idea where we are.'

'I don't think we came too far away from town, maybe three or four miles. I was looking for road signs, but there weren't any - maybe they took them down,' said Robert.

'I think we are going to have to sneak out later. Hopefully, they go to bed early. It's not like there's a telly or anything. As long as we get to the station by midnight, we'll be OK,' whispered Lucy, breaking off as Martha entered the room carrying two mugs of tea.

'Sit yourself down,' said Martha, looking at Robert and gesturing towards the rocking chair, 'Don't you go worrying about it being Joe's chair; he mostly sits in the kitchen anyway. We don't normally light this fire so early in the day, so you might as well make the most of it. It's not like it's Sunday or anything! But don't be putting any more coal on because we will let it go out now. It's taken the chill off, and I don't want you under my feet while I'm preparing the dinner. After we've had a spot of dinner, Joe'll show you round. We all muck in here; you'll have to earn your keep, you know, especially since that fool of a son went and joined the navy. Drink your tea before it gets cold,' and with that, she put the cups down on a small table next to the rocking chair and returned to the kitchen.

'Gosh, she's a fierce one,' whispered James. 'I wouldn't like to cross her!'

***

Several miles away from the three Baxter children, their uncle Archie was sitting on his prison bed, rubbing his eyes.

'I must have dozed off again,' he murmured to himself before looking around at his surroundings. 'I see, so I'm back in 1940, am I?' He jumped up as he heard the key turn in the lock to see two soldiers in the doorway. One was the sergeant that he had met earlier. Was it yesterday? He couldn't remember; he was losing all track of time.

'Just thought you might like to know that the top brass are sending someone from London to talk to you. So you had better have some answers ready, matey!' sneered Sergeant Wood. 'Give him his grub then Private; he won't bite!'

Private Raymond Taylor put the plate of bread and cheese on Archie's bed, keeping a wary eye on the prisoner, his fingers holding tight onto his rifle.

'That's your lot for today. Make the most of it,' said Sergeant Wood.

'Shame to waste good food if they are just going to shoot you,' stammered Private Taylor.

'Now then,' replied the sergeant, 'We won't be shooting him until after he's been found guilty…' turning towards Archie, 'So like I said, you had better have some answers matey.' As they left the room, Archie suddenly realised how hungry he was.

'The trouble with all this time travel is that I keep on missing meals,' he said to himself as he took a big bite from his bread.

Back at the farm, the children were just finishing their meal. It wasn't exactly fine dining. The meal was mostly eaten in silence and consisted of an enormous mountain of mashed potato mixed up with tinned meat, with a generous portion of boiled cabbage on the side. Lucy was prepared for some tricky questions and was busy fabricating a 1940s version of her life, but she was surprised to find that neither Martha nor Joe had the slightest interest in the background of their new guests. James had more practical problems; he was hungry. He had sneaked over to the sink and had borrowed a spoon, holding it until it turned invisible. Then, crouching between Robert and Lucy, he used the technique that he had perfected in the Food Hall of the shopping centre in Cambridge on the day that he had first turned completely invisible. He gently scooped a mouthful of food, holding it a fraction above the plate, until it too turned invisible, before shovelling it into his mouth. He was rather thankful that Lucy, aware of what was happening, had a small appetite, and when she was offered a second helping, she even accepted, so there would be more food for James.

'Glad you like spuds,' laughed Joe, 'Cause you are going to be planting enough of them this afternoon.'

'Did you say you had a son?' asked Lucy.

'Yes, Billy. Damn fool boy ran off to join the navy, didn't he,' replied Joe.

'Language please!' exclaimed Martha.

'Well, he is a fool; what did he do that for? He didn't have to; farmers are a... what they call it?

'A reserved occupation,' joined in Martha, explaining to Lucy and Robert, 'That means they are not conscripted, like coal miners.'

'Anyway, we're farmers. My dad was a farmer; his dad was a farmer; we belong on the land, we live nowhere near the sea.' replied Joe. 'What's the silly fool want to do joining the navy and floating about in a boat for? Well, I reckon war will be over soon, and he can come back and dig his share of potatoes. Right, you two finished? You, young man, can come and give me a hand with the spuds, and you, young miss, what's your name again?'

'Lucy.'

'Right, you can give Martha a hand to clear up, and

then I've got some eggs wants washing. But first, young man, you can help me carry a mattress from upstairs into the barn where you will be sleeping tonight.'

Three hours later, three very tired children were sitting on a bale of hay in the barn comparing their afternoon's work. Lucy had spent the first part of the afternoon on her hands and knees; she'd had to scrub and mop the kitchen floor. She was puzzled by the fact that there was only one tap, a cold tap, above the kitchen sink.

Holding up her bucket, she asked, 'Where's the hot water?'

'Where do you think it is?' replied Martha scornfully, 'In the kettle, of course.' It dawned on Lucy, who had lived all her life in houses with central heating, hot and cold running water, and baths and showers on demand, that this house had no such luxuries. In fact, she realised now, when she took her case upstairs to her new bedroom, she hadn't noticed a bathroom at all. Robert had asked where there was a toilet and had been directed to a brick outhouse outside, but she had presumed, quite wrongly, that there would be another one upstairs. When the floor was dry, she had to rub a red polish into the tiles. After this, she was taken out to one of the barns, where she had to wash eggs in a very cold pail of water and stack them in cardboard trays.

'Don't you dare break any of them mind. There's a war on you know, one egg a month is the ration for people in the town; you think yourself lucky that you come to stay on a farm!' As Martha returned to the farmhouse Lucy, had continued washing the eggs, feeling far from 'lucky.'

'Oh, my back aches,' cried Robert.

'And mine!' echoed James. Robert would have struggled to keep up with the work required from him had it not been for the help that his invisible brother was able to give him. Whilst Joe rode up and down the potato field in his rusty red tractor, ploughing long even furrows into the field, Robert and James followed, planting seed potatoes into each furrow. Having spent much of the afternoon bent double, the two boys were now suffering the consequences.

'I don't think I'll join you for tea,' groaned James, 'It's alright for you, you're fit and sporty, but I'm not built for this. I'm just going to stay here.'

'I'll try and bring you some food back,' said Robert.

'Thanks. So what's the plan?' asked James.

'Well, we've definitely missed our first slot to travel back,' replied Lucy, 'But we have another slot at midnight. Does anyone know where we are and how long it might take us to get to the station?'

'Actually, I do,' said Robert with a very smug look on his face. 'I don't know if you remember, James, but when we were in the potato field, we heard the sound of a train.'

'Yes, I do remember, a steam train!'

'So I figured we were close to the railway line, which is a good thing, as we're trying to get to the station. So, when we were planting the potatoes at the far end of the field, I looked over the hedge, and I saw a tree that I recognised....'

'A tree!' exclaimed Lucy and James incredulously.

'Yes, believe it or not, it's a tree, an oak tree. It's probably been growing there for a hundred years. I know it from the cross-country run. During a run, you come off the track, just before the tunnel, then you run around that tree and follow the footpath back across the fields to the school. I think we are only a couple of miles away from our old school and about an hour away from the station.'

'Surely we can't walk along the railway tracks!' said Lucy, 'What if there are night trains?'

'We don't have to; there's a road that follows pretty much the same route. We didn't come that way, because we came from the centre of town and not from the station, which is on the edge of town. I'm pretty sure the road passes nearby that oak tree. I've been down it just once, on a bike. It's a bit twisty, so the buses don't go that way. That's why you probably don't know it, but I reckon it's our safest bet.'

'So if we leave by ten, we should have enough time,' said Lucy.

'Has anyone got a watch?' asked James.

'No, but there's the clock on the fireplace. It was quite loud when it chimed. I'm sure I'd be able to hear it upstairs. I'll sneak out and join you two,' replied Lucy.

The children were surprised how quickly the evening passed. They had thought that time would drag as they counted off the minutes until they could make their escape, but the novelty of the experience had the opposite effect. After a simple meal of bread and cheese, the Baxters all found themselves separated. James spent the whole evening fast asleep in the barn, lying on a lumpy horsehair mattress, resting on a stack of hay bales. Lucy stayed in the kitchen and, after helping to clear away the dishes from the meal, found herself having a conversation about knitting.

'What? You don't know how to knit?' asked Martha incredulously.

'No, I'm afraid I never learned how to'.

'Well, I don't know what your mother was thinking of. Fancy not knowing how to knit! Well, you are just going to have to learn,'

Martha bustled off to get her knitting basket. The

next two hours flew by as Lucy struggled to master the art of knitting.

Meanwhile, Robert was sitting in one of the armchairs, and Joe was sitting in his rocking chair. There was very little conversation between them because they were both listening intently to the large brown radio that sat on a table in the alcove by the fireplace. They were listening to a comedy show, but Robert was struggling to find it as funny as Joe did, who roared with laughter at the many catchphrases, often repeating them.

'*Anything you fancy sir, go on, anything you like?*' said a lady on the radio called Tilly, who was working in a cake shop.

'Anything you fancy, sir?' laughed Joe. 'I knew that one were coming. She were working in a butcher's last week. You should have heard what she said about the sausages!'

'*Well, it would be silly not to,*' said Major Goodtime, later in the programme, taking yet another opportunity to have a glass of sherry.

'It would be silly not to,' laughed Joe, 'I'll have to remember that one when I'm down the pub.'

Later, Robert was again perplexed listening to the news. He was hoping to learn what was happening in the war. He was used to seeing war reports in far-off lands on the news: brave cameramen with footage filmed on the front line; the shaky images from mobile phones filmed by tourists accidentally caught up in a conflict somewhere; the analysis in the TV studio by experts, almost as immediately as events happened. Somehow though, listening to 1940s radio, he couldn't seem to glean anything from the news reports about what was actually happening.

Then, before long, it was time to get ready for bed. Lucy and her brothers differed in their bedtime rituals. Lucy loved to have a long soak in a bubble bath but would usually wash her hair in the morning. Robert and James, however, always opted for a shower in the morning. Unfortunately, neither option was available to them that evening. There was a pan of water boiling on the stove. Robert had to pour half of it into a large ceramic jug for Lucy to carry upstairs to her room, where there was a matching bowl decorated with bands of pretty roses. Robert poured the rest of the water into a tin basin. He had to strip to the waist in the kitchen and, with the aid of a scrubbing brush and a big block of hard and grainy soap, he attempted to remove the majority of the dirt he had picked up in the potato field

.

***

With five minutes to spare, Lucy crept down the stairs. She was thankful that, on her way up to bed, she had noticed that the third and the seventh step creaked, so she made sure she avoided those. She was worried that she would find the door locked and that she would be unable to get out, but she had no cause to worry. The door was unlocked and hardly made a sound as she slipped outside. She crossed over to the barn and was pleased to find that Robert was already waiting just inside the doorway. Beside him, although of course, she couldn't see him, James was ready too.

'We'll follow you, Robert,' whispered Lucy,

It was a dark night. The moon was obscured by clouds and there was a cool breeze whipping around their bare legs. The children set off walking briskly down the lane.

'I wish leggings had been invented in 1940,' said Lucy. 'My legs are freezing!'

'There's the tree,' said Robert, pointing to a large oak tree looming up out of the darkness, 'The lane that takes us to the station should be opposite. I think it should take us about 40 minutes to get to the station.'

The rest of the journey was uneventful until they were around fifteen minutes away from the town when they became aware of distant noises being carried to them on the night breeze.

'That sounds like thunder!' exclaimed Lucy, 'Do you think it's going to rain?

'Hmm! Maybe. It doesn't really feel like it's going to rain though,' replied Robert as they rounded a bend to have their first sight of Anchester.

'Look!' cried James, pointing towards the town. They couldn't see where he was pointing to, but they didn't need to because the town of Anchester was silhouetted against a red sky.

'What is it?' gasped Lucy, 'It's too late for sunset, and it's too early for dawn.'

'I don't know, but we've just got to press on,' replied Robert. 'We have to make that 12 o clock deadline.'

As they turned the corner of the road that led to the station, they were met with a sight that both shocked and terrified them. The first thing that greeted their eyes were flames leaping from the roof of the red-brick building next to the station. The street, which they had expected to be deserted, was full of people rushing in all directions. A fire engine blocked off part of the road, and jets of water arced into the sky but seemed to make little difference to the burning building. The children approached the station itself but the entrance was blocked by a policeman.

'Where do you think you are going?'

'We have to get to the waiting room.'

'Well, you can't. It's off-limits. Anyway, there will be no trains because, apart from this little mess, a bomb has landed on the railway track.'

'A bomb?'

'That's right, the Jerries probably got lost and turfed out their load before heading back. Anyway, what are you doing out? You should be at home. What are your parents thinking of letting you wander around the streets at night? Don't you know there's a war on? Clear off!'

Robert and Lucy suddenly felt James tugging them back towards the station wall.

'You wait over there,' he whispered, 'In the shadows behind the telephone box, 'I'll go and investigate. Don't worry. I'll be very careful.'

Robert and Lucy did as James asked. Five minutes later, he was back.

'It's no use,' he said, 'The waiting room is full of people. I think it must be the family from the house that's on fire. Maybe it's the stationmaster. Anyway, even if we could sneak in, we couldn't get to the window seat because there's a baby wrapped up in blankets asleep on it, and its mother is sitting next to it. There is no way we would be able to move them.'

'Oh no,' chorused Lucy and Robert.

'We'll have to go back. I think we are stuck here!'

CHAPTER SEVEN

'Well, it looks like we are going to be stuck with you a little while longer,' said Private Raymond Taylor, as he brought in a bowl of watery grey porridge for Archie's breakfast. 'The Jerries were busy last night, the stationmaster's house got bombed, and a bomb hit the railway tracks, so the chap from London who was coming up to interrogate you, sorry, I meant interview you, has turned back and gone home.'

Archie didn't answer; he just shook his head, aware that he no longer seemed in control of events that affected both his own future and the health and wellbeing of his nephew James. He would have been even more concerned if he had realised that, at that very moment, just a few miles away, the children were being roused after a fitful night's sleep.

Lucy felt Martha's firm hand gripping her arm and shaking her...

'Now then, you've slept long enough. Who do you think you are, Sleeping Beauty? You can come down and help me with the breakfast, and tomorrow you better set an alarm clock.'

Lucy groaned as she sat up, not just because she was desperately tired after the night's exertions but also because the rough awakening confirmed that it was still 1940, and she had no idea how they were going to get back to their own time.

The boys' awakening was no gentler.

'Oi! Get up!' shouted Joe, banging on the barn door with a shovel. He then opened the door slightly and allowed the sheepdog that was following him to rush in. If Robert had not been woken by the loud noise, he certainly would have been by the experience of his face being licked by a sheepdog with extremely bad breath. Robert was still dressed in the clothes from the night before, and he sprang to his feet. If James had hoped that his invisibility would allow him to continue sleeping, he quickly realised that he was presented with a new problem because the dog clearly sensed his presence and began barking at him.

Joe opened the door fully.

'What's going on?' and seeing his dog Jet barking at an empty corner of the barn, he cried, 'Oi! Jet! Come here!'.

A very relieved James gingerly sidled up to his brother and gave him a squeeze on the arm as the dog reluctantly backed out of the barn and joined his master.

'What's come over you? Stupid dog!' muttered Joe as he wondered whether there were rats in the barn. He decided to keep that problem to himself. Perhaps not let the dog in there at the same time as the boy, so the boy wouldn't suspect.

'Breakfast should be ready, and then we've potatoes to plant.'

'I'll bring you some food back,' whispered Robert to his brother.

After breakfast, Robert slipped back into the barn.

'James, are you there?'

'Yes, I'm here.'

'Can't stop; I've smuggled out what I could; it's here in my pocket. A bit squashed, I'm afraid. Some bread and jam and some scraps of bacon. We've got to go and help with the potatoes, but I think we're back for lunch.'

'Don't worry. I will come out and find you to help after I have had this.'

Robert left the barn and headed for the tractor where Lucy was already huddled up in the corner of the trailer, tired and despondent and dreading the prospect of a hard morning's work in the potato field. Normally, Jet would leap onto the back of the trailer, but this morning Joe felt a little guilty about the possibility of Robert spending his nights sleeping in a barn with rats running free, so he took Jet over to the barn, ushered him in and closed the door behind him. As he walked back to his trailer, he heard the sound of Jet barking and smiled.

'That will sort the little beggars out.'

The morning wasn't going to plan for James. Before he was halfway through his breakfast, he was faced with a growling, barking, and very confused sheepdog. James gathered up his breakfast, an action that further confused Jet because he noticed the remnants of cold bacon lying on a handkerchief, then gradually disappearing from sight. More worrying for Jet was the fact that he could clearly sense another presence in the barn. He could smell someone, he could hear someone, but couldn't see anyone.

James froze, partly out of fear but also because he wasn't at all sure what he should do. Making a bolt for the door was out of the question because Jet barred the way. Very slowly, James edged his way sideways, hoping that Jet would move away from the door, but Jet remained rooted to the spot. Jet's barking gradually changed to a rhythmic, insistent bark, less aggressive but still very noisy. James also heard the noise of the tractor starting up and driving off towards the potato field, and he realised that, apart from Martha, who was probably inside the farmhouse, he was all alone. He needed a different plan of action.

James had very little experience with dogs. Years spent living in a boarding school had meant that, although he liked animals, he had never had a pet. What he did know, though, was that dogs like being stroked, and they like food. Stroking at the moment was out of the question, but food was a possibility. James felt in his pocket for the remnants of his breakfast and tore off a small piece of bacon. He decided that he had to take the risk that Martha would not come out to the barn and that he could speak.

'Jet, Jet, good dog, good dog, do you want some breakfast?'

There was a pause in the barking as the bewildered dog looked around to see where the voice was coming from. James threw the small piece of bacon halfway between himself and Jet. Gradually the bacon appeared before the dog. Cautiously, he approached and, fearing it might disappear as quickly as it had arrived, quickly snatched it up. James repeated this process twice more, so gradually, the dog got closer and closer to him. The barking had stopped now. Then, with Jet only a few feet away, James held out his hand with the invisible piece of bacon in his palm. All the time, in soothing tones, James was talking…...

'Who's a good doggy? Who's a good doggy? '

Once again, Jet approached cautiously. He could pinpoint exactly where the voice was coming from, there was nothing wrong with his hearing, and he could also pinpoint where there was a piece of bacon; even though he couldn't see it, there was nothing wrong with his sense of smell. Carefully, he reached forward and took the piece of bacon from the outstretched hand and, at the same time, James reached forward and patted him on the back.

'I think I've made a friend, haven't I?'

Over the next ten minutes, little by little, Jet finished off the rest of James' breakfast. By the end, James was sitting on the floor, with Jet sprawled across him, oblivious to the fact that he couldn't see where the food was coming from, nor could he tell who was tickling him behind the ears. What Jet also did not realise was that, because so much of him was now in contact with James, he had now also gradually become invisible.

'That's interesting,' thought James, 'He'll get a shock if he tries to chase his tail; he won't be able to see it!'

***

Half an hour later, James joined Robert and Lucy in the potato field. As Joe and his tractor were at the other end of the field, ploughing deep furrows into the earth, James didn't have to worry about speaking out loud.

'Hello, you two.'

'Well, you took your time,' said Robert.

'Yes, what kept you?' complained Lucy.

'Oh! That's not fair,' replied James, 'Apart from the fact that I had to walk here, I didn't get a lift in a trailer like you, then I had the minor inconvenience of having to calm down a savage dog!'

'I'm sorry,' replied Lucy, 'We're just really tired. It's such hard work. What happened?'

'Well, let me help, and I will tell you all about it.'

Joe looked over to the far side of the field, where he could see Robert and Lucy stooped over, planting potatoes in the trenches that he had ploughed. If he had been nearer, he might have seen a row of potatoes appearing in the trench alongside the two children, the potatoes that James was planting, and he might have heard the tale that James was recounting about his adventures taming the savage beast, Jet. Of course, Robert and Lucy were used to the way that James' imagination tended to elaborate and exaggerate the truth for dramatic effect. In fact, they were rather grateful because it made a backbreaking day's work pass by much more quickly.

Finally, another hard day was over. After their meal, the three children gathered in the barn, giving them the opportunity to pass on to James the food that they had saved from their own plates, plus a few scraps that James could feed to Jet, should they have another encounter.

'So, do we have a plan, Lucy?' asked Robert.

'Not exactly. I think we have to do what we set out to do and that's find Uncle Archie. He is the key to it all. He's the only one who can get us back to our own time and the only one who can help James. I do think, though, that we can't go rushing around the countryside just yet. If we go missing, someone will come looking for us. We are just going to have to stick it out here for as long as it takes and keep our ears open.'

'Yes, we know Uncle Archie came to this area,' said Robert, 'Surely someone must have met him.'

'Archie may be the key,' said James dramatically, 'But I

am the secret weapon!'

'What do you mean?'

'Look, as Lucy said, if you two go wandering around when you are supposed to be on the farm, it will attract attention, but if I go off investigating, no one will miss me, because no one knows I am here and no one can see me anyway.'

'He has a point,' said Robert.

'I could just go off for half days. I could give you a hand with the chores and go off in the afternoons. I know the way we walked into town now, so I could just snoop around.'

'There's something else,' said Lucy, 'I overheard Joe and Martha talking. He said that he was going to be getting a couple of "Land girls", whatever they are, next week because we were going to have to go to school.'

'School!' cried James and Robert in unison.

'Well, that settles it,' said James. 'No point me going back to school. All the more time for me to look for Uncle Archie!'

For the rest of the week, life settled into a pattern. After breakfast, all three children would climb onto the trailer, followed by Jet, who would leap on and immediately seek out his new friend James, who always saved a few scraps of breakfast for him. Then Joe would take them to a field, where they would carry on planting potatoes. Most of the time, instead of going to sleep in the back of the trailer, Jet would trot alongside James, appreciating the fuss that James would make of him.

Lunch was usually thick wedges of homemade buttered bread with a chunk of cheese. The children would sit on the back of the trailer. Luckily, the portions were generous, and there was enough for James to share. Quite often at school, they would have had an apple or a banana with their lunch, or perhaps a yogurt.

'Banana?' Martha had laughed when Robert had dropped a hint that he fancied one, 'Are they eating bananas down in that London of yours then? You must be kidding me. No one has seen a banana for a long time. Mr Hitler and his U-boats have put paid to that!'

'What's a U-boat?' whispered Lucy to Robert moments later.

'A German submarine. They used to sink the merchant ships'

The afternoon brought more work for Robert and Lucy, work that was a direct consequence of the blockade on British merchant ships by the U-boats. Lucy explained the situation to James:

'Because the ships can't bring in all the imported food that they used to, we've got to grow more at home. Did you notice those Dig for Victory posters at the station? Well, it's us that have to do the digging! In the afternoons, we've got to start clearing and weeding that overgrown patch of ground behind the barn, so it can be turned into a kitchen garden. Joe and Martha want to become more self-sufficient because of the food shortages. So maybe that will be a good time for you to go into town and start listening to conversations that might help us track down Uncle Archie. Please be careful, though.'

***

The door to the butcher's shop was held wide open.

'After you,' said a cheery lady from inside the shop to an older lady with a stick, who nodded her approval of the first lady's good manners.

'No, after me!' thought James as he quietly slipped in before her and took a position in the corner of the shop, well out of the way of the growing queue. It was his second afternoon in the shop; an afternoon spent listening to the grumblings and the gossip from the good ladies of Anchester.

'Dearie me, just look at the queue.'

'All this queuing for a tiny bit of meat.'

'It's all that time messing about with coupons and Ration Books causes it.'

'Well, all I can say is it's a good job my George isn't here because he wouldn't be happy with just one sausage for his tea.'

'You had a letter back from him luv?'

'No, he's not one for writing, and he's probably got other things on his mind, what with Mr Hitler and all of that.'

'Well, no news is good news is what I say'…

Two hours later, James quietly left the butcher's shop. He felt he had learned much about the mood of the country. If the ladies of Anchester were a cross-section of women up and down Great Britain, there was a general air of optimism and an intention to get on and make the best of things. They were optimistic, James thought, largely because they had no real idea what was happening in the war. They took at face value the reports they read in newspapers and heard on the radio, but, 'Why not?' he said to himself, 'Better to be happy and busy and supportive, rather than wallowing in self-pity and misery.' As for the mood of the menfolk, well, James had not come across any in the butcher's shop, apart from the elderly butcher himself, who seemed cheerful enough. He never stopped whistling. James was beginning to acquire a knowledge of wartime popular songs and was not altogether impressed! As for any information that would be useful to them, James had drawn a blank so far. The weekend lay ahead then, on Monday, he thought he would try the greengrocer's whilst, for Lucy and Robert, it would be the first day of school.

***

Saturday was a dreary slog. James stayed to help Robert and Lucy with the task of clearing the ground for the vegetable garden. James could take over the digging from Lucy as long as she kept a careful watch in case Joe or Martha appeared. The sight of the earth turning itself over with no one in sight would have been truly alarming for them. Lucy crouched down, picking out the weeds from the soil and laughing at James who was now making aeroplane noises as the worm he was holding seemingly flew through the air and, like everything he touched, slowly became invisible before re-appearing again once he had let it go at Lucy's feet. James had been experimenting with his strange powers. It seemed that he only had an effect on moveable objects, not on fixtures such as doors, or walls or fences. A consequence of this was that Jet, the sheepdog, who now was totally accepting that James' presence was only marked by his smell, not by his sight, loved to jump up and sit on James' knee, whereupon he would slowly disappear. Then, when he jumped off again, he would re-appear mid-flight. The first time he did this, poor Lucy shrieked in surprise and was then forced to mumble an excuse to Martha (who was in the farmyard at the time) about being scared of a bee. Now though they were alone, Lucy looked up from her growing pile of weeds....

'I don't know about you, Robert,' she said. 'But I'll be glad when we have to go to school on Monday. I don't think I can take another week of this.'

'Well, I can't believe I am saying this, but yes, I'll be pleased when I am back at school too!' he replied.

'We have got the day off from farm work tomorrow,' said Lucy. 'Only, Martha was saying that we've all got to go to church tomorrow morning. She said all the evacuees will be there.

***

Lucy twisted her head to look at the rest of the congregation. She had never been in this church before, as her school had its own chapel, but she imagined the interior of the building would look much the same were she to visit it over seventy years later in her own time. On the other hand, the congregation would look very different. For a start, the church was very full, almost bulging at the seams because its ranks had been swelled by the addition of the other evacuees from the town, many of whom Lucy recognised from the day they had arrived at the station. The difference in fashion made the most impact, though because, unlike James, who had been visiting the town and had begun to get more used to the look of 1940s Britain, Lucy had not left the farm (that is, apart from their midnight, thwarted attempt to get back home). All around her was a sea of dark, sombre colour. Some of the older ladies in the congregation looked like they came from an era much earlier, with their coats buttoned up high and tight and hair scraped back beneath an array of different hats and bonnets. She could see that Robert beside her was feeling uncomfortable. His collar was still a little damp because it had only been sponged clean the night before and hung up beside the dying embers of the fire. Living with so few clothes to choose from was proving difficult. She was not as fashion-conscious as some of the girls in her school but, whilst she spent a lot of time in school uniform, at least she had a choice of clean clothes to wear. For both her and Robert, trying to combine the chores they were given around the farm with trying to keep clean was almost impossible. The reason Robert was having to suffer the discomfort of wearing a damp collar was because he had made the mistake of wearing the shirt that he should have kept for his Sunday best the day before. Martha generally wore a pinny to protect her clothes and was surprised that Lucy had not brought one with her.

'Well, we will have to get the Singer out and knock you one up,' said Martha. At first, Lucy had no idea what Martha had meant. It wasn't until Lucy had peeked inside a wooden case that she had seen in the parlour that she understood. It had a curved top and the word 'Singer' emblazoned on the side in gold script, and inside she had discovered a sewing machine. A black machine with ornate decoration and a large wheel on its side. She realised that you had to turn the wheel to make it work.

'Whoever welcomes you welcomes me, and whoever welcomes me welcomes the one who sent me,' intoned the vicar, standing at the pulpit at the front of the church. Lucy forced herself to stop daydreaming about the sewing machine that she was quite looking forward to learning how to use and instead tried to concentrate on the sermon because it was, after all, intended to welcome all the new evacuees to the town.

'Whoever welcomes a prophet in the name of a prophet will receive a prophet's reward, and whoever welcomes a righteous person in the name of a righteous person will receive…'

'Ouch!' gasped Lucy as she felt a sharp poke in her back, followed by smothered giggles from the pew behind. The vicar looked up to see who had disturbed his sermon, then, realising the congregation before him was just a blur, he removed his reading glasses and scanned those before him. By then, although several others were also trying to work out where the sound had come from, Lucy had composed herself and was staring resolutely at the floor. The vicar then replaced his glasses and continued with the sermon. Robert had seen out of the corner of his eye what had happened and turned to look at the occupants of the pew behind them. He recognised two of them instantly. They were two of the mischievous boys that had been playing tag in the railway station just after they had arrived. Either side of them sat two boys who Robert presumed were from the host family. They all looked a similar age to Robert but, whilst the evacuees were scrawny with pinched faces, the local boys were muscular and tall. One of these must be the culprit. Robert pointed a finger in what he hoped was an accusatory and threatening gesture. The response was less than satisfactory, the evacuees pulled faces at him, and the local boys simply glowered menacingly. Robert turned back to face the front, his heart thumping because although he was a sportsman with an athletic body, once away from the playing field, he had a very calm and placid nature.

Ten minutes later, they all filed out of the church. Robert and Lucy were grateful that there were no further incidents with the boys from the pews behind and waited to the side of the church path whilst Martha chatted with one of the other churchgoers. Meanwhile, Joe strode off back in the direction of the farm. Not a regular churchgoer, he was there under sufferance and was keen to get back home.

'Hiya,' whispered James, who had been waiting outside, 'How was it?'

'Okay, until one of those boys there poked me in the back and everyone looked around when I cried out', said Lucy, discreetly gesturing towards the boys in question, who were in the process of being scolded for playing leapfrog over the gravestones.

'Right, I'll go and poke them myself,' said James.

'No, please don't,' replied Lucy, 'I don't want any more trouble.'

'Well, I will go over there and take a closer look at them,' said James, 'Don't worry, I'll keep my distance.'

A few minutes later, Martha joined them.

'And what was you doing making a commotion in the service?' she asked. 'I didn't know where to look!'

'Oh, I'm sorry,' said Lucy, 'I had a sudden pain… Who are those boys over there?'

'Well, two of them's evacuees, but the others are the McGreggor family. They're a rum lot. I'd keep away from them if I were you. There are rumours about how they keep their pigs. Martha nodded towards another family that had wandered over to the McGreggors, 'And them's just as bad…The Munros. I'm surprised Jimmy Munro has made it to church. He's usually in bed of a Saturday, nursing a hangover. He's a farm labourer when he's not in the pub. A rum lot indeed! Well, best be getting back.'

Lucy and Robert looked over to scrutinise Jimmy Munro more carefully. He was a big, scruffy man with a tweed cap pulled over unkempt hair, hair that looked like it had not been in contact with a comb for several days. His wife and son, by contrast, were both small and slight. With them were two more evacuees. Lucy recognised them as being the other two boys who were playing tag in the station on the day they arrived. Lucy and Robert followed Martha down the church path, hoping that James would see them leave and catch them up on the walk back to the farm.

Five minutes later, lagging behind Martha, Lucy and Robert felt a tap on the shoulder. It was James.

'Can't say I cared for that lot, and I am afraid to say that they don't much care for you,' he said. 'They saw you looking over, and one of them said that he had marked your card.' That doesn't sound good.'

'Oh dear!' said Lucy.

'Anyway, I've learned their names, well, their first names anyway. There's the group that were sat behind you in church, the evacuees are called Harry and Mike, and the local lads are Jack and Kevin.'

'Jack and Kevin McGreggor,' added Robert.

'Is that so?' replied James, 'And in the other family that came over, they call the little lad Spike, and the two evacuees are Fred and Pete.'

'Let's hope we can stay out of their way. They look a formidable gang,' whispered Robert.

After lunch, Robert, James and Lucy found they had no chores to do and wanted to make the most of their last free time before school in the morning.

'There's no point going into town because everything will be shut,' said James. 'I took a walk in that direction when you were in church, but I quickly saw that everything was closed up. In any case, it isn't like what we are used to. There aren't places to go for kids our age. It's not like there's a shopping mall and shops selling clothes or CDs or computer games. You can't sit in a coffee shop or order a burger or a smoothie. I remember now that the term 'teenager' doesn't exist yet. I know that from the director of a school production of *Grease* that I was in. It wasn't until the 1950s and Rock & Roll that our generation had its time.'

'Well, I need to get away from the farm', said Robert. 'It's OK for you. You've been free to wander around town all week. We've been stuck here!'

'How about we go to school?' said Lucy, 'Not the school in town that we go to tomorrow, but why don't we have a walk and take a look at our own school, at Greystones?'

An hour later, they were sitting on a fallen log surveying the scene before them from the small copse on the hill that overlooked Greystones.

'Wow!' gasped Lucy, 'It looks so different. I mean, the main building looks almost the same (well, the windows are a different colour), but the new science block isn't there, or the gym, or the dormitories.'

'The sports fields aren't there either,' said Robert. 'Look, there's no cricket pavilion or running track. In fact, there are trees where the football pitch should be. I can see a tennis court, but only one, and it's a lawn court, whereas we have got six hard courts now.'

'It's funny seeing smoke coming out of the chimneys,' said James, 'I wonder who lives there? Oh, look! Something's happening.'

Just then, a bus painted a drab military green swung around the corner and pulled up to Greystones. The large oak front door opened, and three women stepped out. They appeared to be in a uniform, but not one that the children recognised. They had shorts, long socks and khaki pullovers. The women who tumbled out of the bus certainly weren't wearing uniform and wore an array of different-coloured dresses that looked oddly out of place. Holding onto small suitcases, they formed a line and then, with much giggling, they were led inside the house, and the bus that brought them coughed into life and slowly pulled away.

'Well, that was odd!' said Robert, 'So I suppose they are going to be living there. Well, we'd better get going.

We'll have to go back the long way again. We can't take the shortcut along the railway track because can you hear that? It's a steam train. They must have repaired the railway tracks that got damaged during the bombing. We'd better get back and get our stuff ready for school. Are you coming with us to school, James?'

'No, I'll go back into town and see if I can pick up any news about where Uncle Archie might be. You can check out the layout of the school and see if there are any safe places I could sit without getting trampled on in the future.'

'Future,' echoed Lucy, 'How long are we going to be stuck here? How do we get back home to the future?'

***

'Cup of tea, sir?' asked Private Raymond Taylor as he plonked an enamel mug of tea down on Sergeant Wood's desk. 'So what's happening with matey boy in the cells then? I thought they were sending someone up from London to interview him.'

'I don't know, the trains are getting through now, but the chap who was coming has been sent out to France, poor blighter. It's not going so well out there, they say. I think his replacement is up in Edinburgh, so we are just going to have to wait it out. We are not to ask him anything.'

'Never mind, there's worse jobs. Hey Sergeant, you know I'm a trumpet player in a band, the Reg Dorsey Dance Band. Well, we're playing at the Town Hall next weekend. Are you coming?'

'Well, I'm not sure. Might persuade the Missus, but getting kicked in the shins by a bunch of country farmers ain't my idea of good fun.'

'Oh, it's going to be smashing Sarge, you should hear our new version of *'In the Mood'*, you know, the Glen Miller number. It's going to be a great hit with the girls.'

'In the Mood? ...Girls? Where do you think you are? This is Anchester, remember.'

'No, Sarge, you are forgetting, the Land Army will be invited. Some of them are city girls; they know how to enjoy themselves. I tell you, it's going to be a great night.'

CHAPTER EIGHT

Lucy and Robert stood outside the red-brick Victorian school, both of them worried about the day ahead. Glancing around, they saw other evacuees, also looking apprehensive, who were trying to stay out of the way of a group of boys playing football with some unfortunate boy's school cap. Lucy and Robert recognised the unruly boys from the church, with Spike Munro and Jack and Kevin McGreggor amongst them. Then the school door opened, and an elderly teacher stepped outside and rang a handbell. The football game stopped, and the children started to file in.

'Evacuees!' shouted the teacher, 'Form a line and follow me.'

Thirty minutes later, Lucy was sitting at a desk looking

across to Robert, who was on the other side of the room. It was the first time she had been in the same classroom as her older brother, but at this school, there was a greater range of ages than she was used to. Whilst she was next to another girl who seemed very nice (another evacuee who was called Mary Ball), she noticed that Robert had been told to sit next to Fred, one of the boys who were at the church. Fred's brother Peter was at the desk in front of him. Lucy had learned from the register that Fred and Peter were the Redmond brothers. She also knew now that the other boys from the incident in church were called Harry and Mike Gibbs. The McGreggor brothers and Spike were sitting behind her at the back of the room.

Everything looked so different from the schoolrooms that Lucy knew. First of all, the room was painted in drab and dark colours. She was used to light, airy rooms with bright colours, noticeboards and lots of posters and pictures displaying information. In many of her classrooms (for she was used to moving from one classroom to another for different subjects), the rooms were arranged with several large desks where pupils sat in groups, often carrying out work as a team. Here, however, they were seated at regimented wooden desks, and it seemed they would be at these desks for all their subjects. The desk and the chair she sat on were fixed together to a metal frame. Thankfully, she had a back to the chair, but it was still very hard and uncomfortable; she couldn't adjust its position. The schoolteacher at the front looked really old, but perhaps that was because all the young teachers were fighting in the war. He wore a black gown that was tatty and threadbare over an equally threadbare jacket. His hair was grey, and he had small spectacles balanced on the end of his nose. The whole class had to chant 'Good Morning

Mr Greville,' when he entered and to call out 'Here sir!' when he marked the register.

Robert stared resolutely ahead. He could see out of the corner of his eye that Fred was pulling faces at him, relying on the poor eyesight of Mr Greville, and this was making his brother, Peter, turn around and smirk at him.

'English books!' shouted Mr Greville, 'Get out your English notebooks.'

Everyone except the evacuees delved into their desks.

'Quietly! Stop banging!' shouted Mr Greville to no avail, as many of the pupils repeatedly opened and shut their desk lids, trying to make as much noise as they felt they could get away with.

'Quietly! Or someone will be feeling my cane across their fingers!' The noise subsided.

'Now listen,' and he started to read aloud from a book: *'What a piece of work is a man! How noble in reason, how infinite in faculty! In form and moving how express and admirable! In action how like an Angel!'* Well? Who wrote that?' He peered over his glasses, waiting for a response. A girl at the front of the class raised her hand.

'Is it Dickens sir?'

'Does it sound like Dickens? No, it is not. Surely one of you numbskulls must know.' Very slowly, both Lucy and Robert raised their hands. Lucy was certain she knew the answer, and Robert, although less confident, thought he knew too because it was a line he had heard James repeat when he was learning his lines for a school play.

'You, boy.'

'Is it Shakespeare, sir?'

'Yes, it most certainly is, and which play, may I ask?' as he looked around the room. This time Lucy's hand shot up because she definitely knew the answer to this, remembering how proud she had been of James in the school production.

'Well?'

'It's Hamlet, sir'

'Good, yes, Hamlet. That is the play we will be reading. This is the book; you will take turns at reading from it, and the rest of you will listen quietly! Seeing you are so familiar with the works of the Bard, you can start.' He handed a textbook to Lucy. As her clear, articulate tones rang out as she read from the book with clarity and comprehension, Robert started to have doubts about their recent actions. They should have been trying to blend in and not draw attention to themselves, but they had achieved just the opposite. He could hear the boys around him start to whisper and mutter to themselves.

'Silence!' shouted Mr Greville, and he ordered Lucy to pass the book to Mary, the girl seated beside her. The whispering only continued when, in contrast to Lucy's, Mary's quiet and shy voice stumbled and slipped over the words, losing all meaning and rhythm.

'Enough!' shouted the teacher as he snatched the book back and passed it to another pupil. Lucy reached across and gave Mary a reassuring squeeze on the arm as soon as she was sure that Mr Greville was not looking, and from that moment, they became friends.

***

James had squeezed himself in at the back of the greengrocer's, out of the way behind some sacks of potatoes, and continued with his vigil listening out for any news that might point the way to where Uncle Archie might be. Whilst nothing he heard seem to have any bearing on their predicament, with his love of drama and his keen ear for different inflexions of speech, it was quite an entertaining way to spend the day.

'Where's your onions gone?'

'They are gone; that's where.'

'Well, when are you going to get some more?'

'I don't know; they used to be imported from Jersey. Can't get them no more.'

'Oh! Got any Jersey potatoes?'

'Are you soft in the head? Do you think our boys in the navy should risk getting sunk just so you can have your bangers and mash?'

'Well, at least sausages ain't rationed.'

'Not yet, they are not, but I bet they will be if this war goes on much longer.'

'Sausages? I tell you what, we had some pork sausages last week, and I swear they had been nowhere near a pig. More like a fried bread roll than a sausage.'

James, listening at the back of the shop, realised from the mention of the ration book that he hadn't witnessed any sign of ration books in this shop. So vegetables weren't rationed. It didn't stop the customers complaining, though, especially about the shortages.

'Got any onions?'

'If I had a pound for every time someone asked me for onions, I would be a rich man!'

'You could afford to get some onions in then. Now then, spuds, you only got them Lincolnshire whites? Where are your Jersey Royals?'

***

At school, English continued for the rest of the morning. As much as Lucy liked Shakespeare, she felt that sitting listening to her classmates reading aloud, without even having a textbook of her own to follow, did not contribute very much to her learning. Robert lost concentration and drifted off into a daydream very quickly, only snapping back into reality shortly before it was his turn to read.

The Geography exercise just before the lunch break was more of a challenge.

'In this time of adversity,' stated Mr Greville, 'It is important that we should stand up and be proud of who we are. So I want you all to write down in your jotters as many countries that form the British Empire as you can remember.'

Robert broke into a cold sweat; his mind went blank, his pencil hovered motionless over his jotter. He could think of the Roman Empire (not that he could remember how far it stretched). He knew there was an Empire in the 'Star Wars' films, but these did not help him at all. He felt a presence behind him, a sensation almost like a weight pressing down on the back of his head. He realised Mr Greville was standing right behind him.

'You, boy! Baxter is it? Why have you not written anything down? Are you a shirker? A do-nothing idler? You are English, aren't you? How do you think we will win the war with that kind of attitude? If you do not give me the name of a country immediately, you will feel my cane, boy!'

Robert's brain raced as he struggled to think of a country that might be in the Empire. Then he remembered something he had seen on the news, some kind of protest with the border between Spain and, and...

'Gibraltar, sir.'

'Gibraltar! Is that the best you can come up with? Gibraltar! A little rock in the Mediterranean? Well, that is not the first country I would have thought of, The only thing that is sparing you the cane is the fact that it is in an important position for our navy and air force, but you should do better, so you, my boy, will stay in over the lunch break and copy out the names of countries from our Empire. Now, you girl, what have you got?'

'India, Malaya, Rhodesia, Jamaica.....'

***

It was lunchtime. James decided he needed a change of scenery and to stretch his legs because he was beginning to get cramp as he crouched behind the potato sacks. At an opportune moment, when the door was pushed open, he slipped out into the sunshine, his eyes blinking at the sudden change from being in the dark depths of the shop. It was because of this momentary blindness that he failed to notice a man come lurching out of the Fox and Hounds and stand on his foot. Amazingly, the man did not seem to notice. James hopped to one side as two matronly women walked in the same direction as the man, who was clearly very drunk. Apart from the fact that he was so unsteady on his feet, his intoxication was accentuated because he had a pronounced limp. James followed the group along the pavement.

'Just look at the state of him, and so early in the day.'

'I know, it's Billy Munro. He oughta be ashamed of himself. His dad's just as bad, I daresay he's still in the pub.'

'You know how he got that limp, don't you?'

'I certainly do; they say he stuck a pitchfork in his foot when war broke out so as he wouldn't have to go and fight.'

'Stupid boy as well as a coward. He's exempt from conscription anyway because he's a farmer.'

'Another Munro', thought James, 'I wonder if he's related to that boy Spike in the churchyard.'

***

At that moment, Lucy and her new friend Mary were pressed to the railings in the playground watching Spike

Munro. He was among the last few boys left in a game of British Bulldog. It was a game that Lucy had never seen before. Mary had explained the rules at the outset when there was just one boy standing in the middle of the playground with most of the rest of the school lined up along the railings facing him.

'They have just got to get to the other side. Any as he catches becomes bulldogs too and tries to catch the rest when they come back.'

Spike was proving to be very adept at the game, he was extremely quick and nimble on his feet, and he would wriggle and weave his way through the pack without being caught. It was far too rough a game for the two girls. Many of the other children came back nursing cuts and bruises, but generally, there were shrieks of laughter. It was clearly a popular game.

Lucy had learned quite a lot about Mary in quite a short time. It seemed Mary was an only child, and her father had been a fisherman who had died in an accident at sea several years before. Her mother still lived by the coast, but because there was a naval base nearby, there was a risk of bombing, so Mary had been sent away. Lucy sensed that Mary wished her mother had moved away with her, but she said her mother had lots of friends at home and didn't want to leave them.

'My mother's nothing like me,' Mary said, 'I'm so shy, but you should see my mother, she's so pretty, and she can dance like a princess. Everybody likes my mother; she's the life and soul of the party.'

Lucy asked Mary how she was enjoying life in Anchester.

'Actually, I've been a bit lonely. The couple I'm staying with are quite elderly and, although they treat me well enough, I have no one to talk to and nothing to do.'

'Well, we have quite a few chores to do around the farm, but when I can, I will come and see you. I like talking to you.'

'no one has ever said that to me before. They usually call me nasty names on account of me not being able to read and write very well.'

'Are you dyslexic?'

'Dis what?'

'Dyslexic, you know, it means that..., oh!' Lucy suddenly realised that dyslexia might be a condition that they did not know about in 1940s Britain and was struggling to think of a way to change the subject when the school bell rang and the moment passed. As they filed in, she realised that she was going to have to think more clearly before she spoke, or she might give the game away.

***

Archie was thinking along similar lines. He was spending much of his time asleep or pretending to sleep so that he wouldn't have to interact with the guards. Only one of them seemed to be chatty anyway, the young private who whistled a lot, but the fewer conversations Archie had, the less likely he was to contradict himself. He had decided he needed to play for time in case there was any possibility that whoever had operated the machine previously might be able to bring him back home. The best plan of action he could come up with so far was to pretend he had amnesia; it may delay things for a while. He tried to exercise his mind by thinking of as many events that happened before the war as he could. He realised that he was on dangerous ground discussing anything directly related to the war because he did not know whether the facts he knew were known by the general public at the time of the war. If he revealed things that he ought not to know, they might suspect that he was a spy and shoot him!

***

Robert was finding his first day at school very stressful and longed for it to be over. He noticed that some of his classmates knew how to manipulate their teacher so that, instead of teaching the lesson, he would begin to reminisce about the time he spent in the trenches during the First World War.

'I enlisted!' he would say proudly, 'I wasn't conscripted, no one had to tell me to go, I enlisted!'

It didn't take much to get him started.

'Was it like that when you were a soldier, sir?' Then his mind was off on its travels back into the past. He would stand at the window, his arms clasped behind his back like an officer, although he was never promoted past the rank of corporal, and he would stare into space and recount his adventures. Meanwhile, behind him, the class would develop into a quiet anarchy. Robert felt a lot of the brunt of this. Paper pellets would thud into the back of his neck, directed by the McGreggor brothers behind him, or Spike Munro would sneak out from the back of the class and jab him in the ribs with a ruler.

***

James continued to be entertained by the banter in the queue in the greengrocer's shop.

'What kind of spuds are them?'

'King Edwards.'

'Have you got any Jersey potatoes?'

'How many times do I have to say. No, we don't; the Nazis are eating all your Jersey spuds.'

'Only I thought now the Land Army have come..'

'Give me strength! What do you expect them to do,

cross the channel, drive a tank into the fields and capture some spuds?'

CHAPTER NINE

James had joined Robert and Lucy as they walked home from school.

'Do you know anything about the Land Army?' asked James, 'Only I heard them mentioned today.'

'Do you think they are the same as the Land Girls?' asked Lucy. 'Do you remember, Martha and Joe said they were coming to the farm?'

'I don't like to ask too many questions,' said Robert, 'I never know what's a stupid question, something that I really ought to know, something that might attract attention.'

Their questions were quickly answered because, as they swung open the farm gates, they were greeted by the sight of two young ladies sat on the farmhouse steps drinking tea from enamel mugs. One was wearing a pair of breeches with long socks and a green jersey. The other girl was dressed in dungarees over a white shirt. Both had brown boots and were wearing cowboy-style brown hats that were positioned in a very jaunty, non-military position on the back of their heads.

'I tell you what Joan,' the one in the dungarees was saying in a broad Birmingham accent, 'This shirt ain't half itchy. They gave us three like this, and they all look as bad as each other.'

'Tell me about it, Jane, ' replied Joan, in an equally broad accent, 'Oh look! We got company! Hello.'

'Hello,' chorused Robert and Lucy.

'I'm Joan, and this is Jane. I tell you what when I joined the Land Army; I didn't reckon it was going to be as hard work as all this.'

'No, I didn't either,' said Jane, 'We thought it would be like having a country holiday. Fancied a change from the city, what with the threat of bombs and all that, but it's blooming hard work. We've been digging all day, and my back's killing me.'

'It's very dirty in the countryside too,' said Joan. 'It gets everywhere.'

Just then, a horn beeped as the same military bus that they had seen at Greystones pulled up outside the farm. The girls jumped up and handed their mugs to Lucy.

'Do us a favour, take them in and swill them out, will you? Don't wanna miss our lift, cos we don't know the way back to Greystones yet. See ya,' and with that, they dashed out of the farm gates and climbed aboard the bus.

'So, now we know who the Land Army are, and we also know who's staying at our school.'

Later, when they were eating, Joe was less than complimentary about his new workforce.

'Land Army! That's a joke; them's a couple of city girls they are. Don't know one end of a spade from t'other. If that damn fool boy of ours hadn't run off to join the navy, we wouldn't need them.'

'Language please!' said Martha.

Robert was pleased that Martha had not wanted him to sleep in her son's room because the time he spent in the barn at the end of the day was important to himself and James: it gave them an opportunity to chat with very little risk of being overheard. This would have been very difficult to do had they all been sleeping inside. James kept Robert amused by impersonating the various people he had been observing in the greengrocer's. However, when he heard about Robert's encounters with the McGreggors and the other boys, who seemed to have formed themselves into a gang of bullies, he was incensed and secretly resolved to pay the school a visit in the morning.

The following day, they all set off in the direction of the school. On the way, they took a detour, so Lucy could knock at the door where her new friend Mary was staying and, at this point, James said goodbye and headed off in the direction of the town centre to continue his search for information about Uncle Archie's whereabouts. However, he intended to visit the school secretly once the day had begun because he knew it was too risky to attempt the visit whilst everyone was milling around in the playground. Someone was likely to bump into him.

After an hour, James grew tired of waiting in the butcher's shop; it was a quiet morning, and he thought it would be a good time to visit the school. He waited outside the school for a while, wondering whether he should risk opening the big black front door himself when eventually he spotted a postman who was carrying a parcel that clearly would not fit through the letterbox. James silently slipped behind the postman, walking as close as a shadow. The postman opened the door, put his sack down, which jammed it open, and stepped inside to put the parcel on a small table in the hallway. Before the postman had turned and retrieved his sack, James was already halfway down the corridor, searching for Robert and Lucy's classroom. It was a small school, and it didn't take him long to find it. The door was closed, but it had a glass window in it, and through it, he could see Robert sitting at a desk at the front of the class.

Inside, Robert was ruminating on the morning's events. The day had begun much as the previous one had ended, with the teacher, Mr Greville, bragging about how brave he had been in the previous war and with the classroom bullies attempting to make life miserable for Robert. Unfortunately, the peace was shattered when Robert, having received a dig in the ribs from Spike Munro, involuntarily let go of the book he was holding, and it skidded across the floor. The noise it made interrupted Mr Greville in full flow, and he spun around, bellowing.

'Who threw that book?'

Robert raised his hand.

'It was an accident, sir.'

'Accident!' screeched Mr Greville. 'Come down to the front, boy. I am going to move you to my 'Hot Seat', where I can keep an eye on you, but first of all, you can stand there and hold out your hand.'

So now Robert was sitting at the front of the class, right in front of Mr Greville's desk. Despite the fact that his fingers were smarting where Mr Greville had whacked them with a ruler, he felt that his situation had improved. It would be much harder for the bullies to reach him where he was now sitting. He was later to discover that he had made some new friends in the class because some of the others realised what had happened and admired the fact that he hadn't 'snitched'.

James, however, was oblivious to what had previously happened, although he was curious to discover why Robert was not sitting in the position that he had described to him the night before. He managed to jump out of the way in time when Mr Greville approached the door and opened it.

'I need more chalk; I don't want to hear any noise from you. I will be back in a second. Any noise and someone else will be feeling my ruler!'

For once, the classroom was relatively quiet, perhaps chastened by watching the punishment inflicted on Robert. James quickly entered the classroom and crouched down next to Robert's desk. Gradually, the noise in the classroom increased to a low hum, and James felt it was safe to whisper to his brother.

'Hello Robert'

'What are you doing here?'

Before James could answer, Mr Greville was back.

'Right, Arithmetic!' shouted the teacher, 'Let's see how good you are with money. You have to work out these sums in your head – just write down the answer in your jotter. We will see who might aspire to getting a job as a clerk in a bank and who is going to end up on a farm digging ditches!'

James quickly realised that this was a new threat to their wellbeing and one to which both Robert and Lucy were oblivious. This was confirmed when he glanced over to where Lucy was, several rows back from where Robert was sitting and could see her waiting expectantly for the next lesson, for she had always been quite strong at maths and wouldn't be put off by the fact that she wouldn't be able to use a calculator. James knew that there was something that he had not got round to telling Lucy and Robert about, and that was that the way money was calculated had changed! Each of them had a few pennies in their pockets when they arrived in the 1940s, and they had remarked on how the coins had changed; they were much bigger and heavier, but there was more to it than that, James knew because he had spent so much time in the shops watching people buy meat and vegetables.

'So, Farmer Brown has three sheep and a ram,' declared Mr Greville, 'He sells the sheep for two pounds ten shillings each, and the ram is worth double one of the sheep. How much does he take home?'

Robert was not as quick at arithmetic as Lucy; he tended to rely on a calculator. For a moment, he forgot that James was in the room as he struggled to work out the sum, but then felt a tap on his hand and looked down to find that James had written the answer in the notebook before him. James, meanwhile, thankful that he had an invisible pencil in his invisible pocket, was already quietly tip toing over to where Lucy was sitting. Lucy had already confidently written the answer down. £10.50. Not realising that James was in the room, she was astonished and annoyed to see her answer scribbled out, and a new one take its place: £12 10s.

'Trust me,' whispered James into Lucy's ear. Lucy, knowing James' love of playing tricks, had little faith in him but had no time to react because she heard Mr Greville bark out:

'I want an answer now. You, girl!' Luckily Mr Greville pointed to a girl on the row behind Lucy, who dutifully answered.

'Twelve pounds ten, sir.'

'Correct, but it costs him half a crown to buy his lunch, so now how much has he got? Quick! You, boy.'

'Twelve pounds seven and six, sir.'

'And two and six to put petrol in his truck. Well?'

'Twelve pounds five shillings, sir.'

Lucy was dumbfounded. It didn't make any sense to her at all. Luckily neither she nor Robert had been asked for an answer. James was in a state of near nervous exhaustion. Not only did he have to dash silently up and down between Lucy and Robert's desks and avoid bumping into the teacher, but he had to do it whilst trying to calculate the answer to the sums. There was a brief moment of respite whilst Mr Greville harangued a boy near the back of the class for failing to give him an answer, and Lucy saw words appear at the bottom of the page of her open notebook:

'12 pennies in a shilling, 20 shillings in a pound.' She covered it with her hand and concentrated on the next sum that Mr Greville was announcing. Meanwhile, James dashed back to Robert's desk to write the same thing in his book. James had taken to giving his brother and sister two taps on the wrist to show he had arrived and one tap to show he was going. He had just finished writing on Robert's notebook when he heard Lucy being asked for the answer to the latest sum. He hadn't heard the question himself, he had relied on them not being asked this time around, but now his sister would be put on the spot!

Lucy's mind raced. It was a good job that she was good at maths because she had to undo all she knew about decimal currency and apply the formula that James had written. It still took her longer to answer than most of her classmates would.

'Well, we haven't got all day?'

'It's one pound and, err, seven p, sir.'

'Pea?' snorted Mr Greville, 'Pea? Who said anything about vegetables? I think living on a farm is making you go soft in the head, girl.' As the other children began to laugh at Mr Greville's remarks, Lucy felt two taps on her wrist and looked down to see another word written on the page before her.

'Sorry, sir, I meant seven pence, sir.' As the laughter began to subside, to the Baxter children's relief, they heard the sound of the school bell ringing out. It was time for lunch. James gave Lucy a tap on the wrist and retreated to the far corner of the room. He didn't want to be crushed if the children made a rush for the door.

'Wait!' shouted Mr Greville, 'Tomorrow afternoon, you will be having PT. Make sure you have suitable clothes and footwear.'

'What's PT?' Robert whispered to the boy in the next desk to him. Stephen Miller looked quizzically at Robert. 'Surely everyone knew that PT. meant physical training?' he thought. 'He can't have meant 'what does it mean?'

'What are we doing? Depends on the weather', he replied. 'We might be playing cricket, but if it rains, we might have to go for a cross-country run, or we might just have to jump up and down and do exercises in the playground.'

James waited for an opportune moment before slipping out of the classroom and finding his brother and sister, who were waiting in a corner of the playground, expecting his arrival. All thoughts of staying to play tricks on the class bullies were gone from his head.

'Hello,' he whispered, 'That was a tough lesson.'

'Goodness!' replied Lucy, 'I had no idea. We need to

do some more work on this tonight. In fact, he's given us some homework; it's about a suit costing two guineas. How much is two guineas?'

'Dunno,' replied James, 'Nothing costs two guineas in the veg shop. I thought I would see if the town library is open this afternoon. I will see if I can find out. Have you saved me some of your sandwich? I'm starving.'

***

'Guinea: The sum of one pound and one shilling.' James read later in the library. The library was empty apart from the librarian, who had looked up from the book she was reading as James made his entrance. As she got up to close the door that she had thought had blown open, James picked up a dictionary that he saw on a shelf in the reference section and ducked behind a desk to wait behind a bookshelf whilst the book turned invisible. Then he nonchalantly walked back to sit on a chair, in the full knowledge that neither he nor the book could be seen by the librarian.

'Idiot!' he thought to himself. It was true that the librarian could not see the pages of the book turning by themselves, but neither could he. This was going to prove a longer exercise. He got up and took the book with him to the back of the room, where he sat on the floor and placed the book back in front of him while he waited for it to re-appear. Then, slowly, he leafed through the dictionary, a few pages at a time, until he arrived at the right page. He had only just read the definition when the librarian appeared around the corner.

'Tsk! Who left that book on the floor?' and she picked it up and, luckily, turned and retraced her steps back to the front of the library. If she had continued in the same direction, she would have tripped over James!

Before he left the library, James took a look at the noticeboard but saw very little that he thought would be of use. He was wrong. A handwritten poster advertising a dance at the town hall on Friday evening with the Reg Dorsey Dance Band was going to prove a very important event for the Baxter children.

The following afternoon, Robert was standing in a line, together with the other boys from his class, looking at the occasional raindrop landing in the puddles that had formed on the playground. Lucy and the other girls had been sent to the hall to do 'exercises'. The boys were to go on a cross-country run and were listening to Mr Greville, who was standing under an umbrella, describing the route.

'It's straightforward. You run to the end of the road and turn left. You climb over the stile, and you follow the footpath in a straight line. You will pass a small wood on your left. When you reach the canal, turn right and then turn left, running down the far side of the woods. This will bring you back all the way to the road that you started on. The winner is the first one back to the playground. All you need to do is to follow Munro. He runs like a hare.'

Robert looked across to Spike Munro, who smiled smugly. The rest of the gang patted him on the back. At last, Robert was in his element. The only thing that concerned him was what he was wearing. Instead of his trainers, he was wearing his school shoes; instead of his running shorts, he was wearing his school shorts and, instead of his fluorescent yellow, sleek, high-performance running vest, he was wearing his beige, woollen under-vest. Still, he would give it his best shot and, in any case, most of the others wore similar clothes.

'On your marks, get set, go.'

Robert decided to pace himself, as the route was new

to him, and slotted himself in the first group of runners, making sure that he didn't let Spike Munro get too far ahead. Spike was clearly a good runner, but Robert was undeterred, for he realised that he had an advantage over Spike. Having had the benefit of a better diet than his wartime counterparts, not only was he stronger than Spike, but he had also the benefit of having had extensive coaching at his school. Not that everyone's diet was inferior in wartime Britain, he thought, as he jogged along. Whilst the range of food available was very limited, and certainly, the range of recipes was equally limited (there were no Chinese, Italian, or Indian foods available, for example), the diet of the children was wholesome and fresh. There were none of the problems associated with 21st-century junk food. He hadn't seen any children who would qualify as obese! At least, living on a farm, they were not short of food, which was a good thing, as there was always plenty to smuggle out for James to eat. As Robert pondered these thoughts, he realised that the others in the leading group had dropped behind, and there was no one between him and Spike Munro. He looked over his shoulder to see how far ahead of the others they were, and he just caught sight of a group of boys entering the wood that they were now passing on their left. The McGreggors were amongst them.

'Cheats,' he thought and then concentrated on his race strategy. Spike Munro was clearly not used to anyone being quite so near to him at this stage of a race and kept anxiously looking behind him. Robert sensed that victory was his for the taking but bided his time and waited until they had run along the canal towpath and then joined the track that would lead all the way back to the road by the school. Now that he was not worried about losing his way, he gradually increased his pace and sailed past Spike Munro.

He knew better than to look back but just focused directly ahead as he passed the woods, steadily increasing his pace to widen the gap between himself and Spike. He was so much at ease with the familiar task of maintaining a regular rhythm to his running that he did not expect what was to happen next. Suddenly, from behind a bush at the edge of the woods, dashed a group of boys; they were the boys he had seen sneaking into the woods earlier. He tried to avoid them, but one stuck out a leg, and he went sprawling, then several of them jumped on top of him and pinned him down.

'See ya later, sucker!' jeered Spike Munro as he ran past them on his way down the track. Robert struggled, but the sheer weight of all the bodies on top of him made it impossible to move.

'Get off him.'

The other runners following had arrived. Kevin McGreggor stood up and faced them.

'And are you gonna make me?'

This change was enough, and, with the rest of the boys distracted, Robert was able to twist over and, pushing the other boys off him, he struggled to his feet. To his dismay, he could see that Spike Munro was now a distant figure on the horizon, but Robert would not give up and, ignoring the jeering and catcalls from behind him, he started once again to run.

It was a lost cause; not only had he lost a lot of time, but the struggle on the floor had taken a lot out of him, and he knew the chances of catching Spike were remote. He came close, though. By the time they reached the school gates, Spike Munro was once again looking anxiously behind at Robert, who was steadily reducing the gap between them. A few minutes more, and he would have made it, but Robert had to be satisfied with entering the school playground in second place.

'A good effort Baxter,' said Mr Greville, 'But you will have to go some to catch our Spike Munro. He's a little harrier!'

***

'What a week!' exclaimed Lucy as they walked back to the farm on Friday afternoon. 'I'm looking forward to sitting by the fire and doing some knitting. I'm also going to be shown how to use the sewing machine. Mrs Sinclair has got some curtains, and we are going to make them into a pinnie. Do you want one?'

'Ha Ha!' replied Robert, 'I do hope that we haven't got a lot of farming chores lined up. I don't mind planting a few seeds on the vegetable plot (after all 'Dig for Victory'), but I hope we don't have to go out in the fields. Let's hope the Land Girls have been pulling their weight.'

'What a week,' echoed one of the Land Girls, Joan, as she washed the mud off her boots at the pump in the farmyard, 'I'll tell you something for nothing, Jane, I'm looking forward to a lie-in tomorrow morning.'

'Well, you need your beauty sleep. After all, we've got a dance to go to tomorrow evening.'

'Oh, I do hope it's not one of them country bumpkin affairs – you know, sitting on hay bales and doing the Do-si-do!'

'No, I don't think so; they are called the Reg summat Dance Band. Doesn't sound like country dancing. Better not be. Had enough of the countryside for one week – it's stuck all over my boots!'

CHAPTER TEN

After James had spent a week listening to gossip in the town, his first lead came to him without any effort. He had not joined Robert and Lucy on their walk to school because it had started to rain, and he had noticed previously that the raindrops looked strange as they bounced off his invisible body. He was lying stretched out on a hay bale at the back of the barn when the two Land Army girls also came into the barn to shelter from the rain.

'Go on, Joan, tell me again about Friday night at the dance. He sounds dreamy.'

'Well, it was after the first break. They had just been playing *In The Mood* when he jumps off the stage and walks straight up to me and offered me a cigarette and says 'Are you in the mood, doll?' Well, that made me laugh, and I told him he'd been watching too many movies, and he asked me if I liked the band, and I told him I did, and I put on my best Hollywood movie voice and said, 'You blow a pretty mean horn sonny,' which made him laugh. Then he asked me if I preferred Count Basie or Duke Ellington, you know, trying to show off his music knowledge, so I told him neither, I preferred Benny Goodman.'

'He's probably never met a city girl before.'

'No, did I tell you, it really made me laugh, I said to him, 'Well, you play alright for a farmer. Do you get the cows to sleep?' Oh, he didn't like that, he didn't. 'Farmer?'… he nearly dropped his cigarette in his beer and said, 'I'll have you know that my job is crucial to the war effort.'

'So what's he do then?'

'He works in a prison. Says he's guarding a Nazi spy. Well, he thinks he's a spy. This chap ain't saying nothing, he's English alright, but he's not from around here, and there's something strange about him, so he probably is a spy. Then he wouldn't say anything else about him. Said he had said too much and *walls had ears*!'

'So when are you seeing him again?'

'Tomorrow after work. We're going for a walk in the park. I'll miss my tea, but he said he would buy me Fish and Chips.'

'Oh, so romantic. What's his name again?'

'Ray. Ray Taylor.'

'Ooh, he's your little ray of light. Look, it's stopped raining, we better get going, or Farmer Joe will be getting in one of his moods!'

James sat up with excitement. At last! Maybe this mystery prisoner was not the right man, but it was the best lead he had had all week. It was going to be hard waiting

STUCK (IN TIME)

until Tuesday. The best thing he could do today would be to go and check out the park and then find the fish and chip shop so he would be fully prepared. For the moment, though, it was raining, and he may as well catch up on some sleep.

***

The next two days passed uneventfully for James. He put all his hope into joining Ray Taylor and Joan on their date and thought there was little point in spending his days wandering around the town. Instead, he helped his brother and sister by doing some weeding on the new vegetable patch. With Joe and the Land Army girls away in the fields and Martha inside the farmhouse, it was a fairly non-stressful activity, and he thought he may as well make the most of the late spring sunshine.

Tuesday evening arrived, and James made sure that he was outside the entrance to the park from early afternoon. He knew he wasn't late because Joan was still working in the field when he set off, but he didn't know if she was going back to Greystones or was being picked up from the farm, and he didn't want to leave anything to chance. He sat on the stump of a recently-felled tree and studied the people who arrived at the park, some with children, some with dogs, but none as yet accompanying Joan. He heard the roar of a motorbike arriving and stopping outside the park - a large black motorbike with a sidecar attached - and he watched the rider dismount and then lean against the park railings smoking a cigarette, running a comb through his hair and straightening his grey uniform. This looked promising. Then, shortly afterwards, a bus pulled up and out jumped Joan, changed from her Land Army uniform into a brightly patterned dress, together with a green cardigan. She stood shyly on the pavement whilst Ray (for

143

it was obviously him) jumped up, stubbed out his cigarette and crossed the road to greet her. They then entered the park, and James sprang up and followed them down the path.

After a few minutes, James began to feel uncomfortable. It was one thing listening in on public conversations in a shop, but it was something else playing gooseberry to a courting couple. Not that their conversation was at all intimate, they both seemed quite shy in each other's company, but it still felt like snooping.

'After all, I don't need to listen to this,' he thought to himself, 'They aren't actually very likely to talk about Uncle Archie, are they? Ray said that he had said too much the last time, and it wouldn't exactly be a very romantic topic of conversation. No, all I need do is keep my distance and keep an eye on Ray. He's the key. I just need to follow him and find out where he works.'

For the rest of the evening, James slowly followed the couple as they ambled around the park. For some of the time, they sat on a park bench, and James did likewise, sitting further down the path. When they stopped to throw some bread to the ducks on the pond, James realised that he was starting to get hungry and felt quite envious of the ducks! Evidently, Ray and Joan were feeling peckish too because he heard Ray jump up and, in a loud voice, imitating a butler or a waiter exclaim:

'Would Madam like to dine now? Can I escort you to the chippy?'

***

Lucy was sitting on Mary's bed trying to help her with

her English homework; they had been asked to describe the street that they lived in before they were evacuated. For Lucy, this presented a problem; she could hardly describe Greystones High School because it would be recognised as the local Greystones Hall and, in any case, no one would believe that she and Robert lived in such a big house. Even the house they were brought up in before their parents went missing might attract attention because it too was quite large, so Robert and Lucy had joined forces, and each described a house that was very familiar to them through watching a soap opera on TV. Lucy had finished her homework before rushing round to Mary's house.

'It's no good, Lucy. I can see in my head so clearly what I want to say. It's like a picture, I know exactly what it looks like, but I can't think of any of the words to describe it.'

'Well, why don't you draw a picture of it first and then write about it?'

'That's a good idea. I love drawing, but I haven't got any spare paper.'

'Oh, I have,' said Lucy, 'have this.' She fished in her bag and drew out a notebook. When she had set off on this journey through time, she had brought a notebook and her school pencil case with her, and all these items had transformed into their 1940s equivalents. Her notebook had lost its shiny printed cover, and the paper was not such good quality, but Mary's eyes opened wide when she saw it.

'Oh Lucy, no, really I couldn't. That's too precious. I could never afford something like that.'

'No, I insist, you must have it, please, take it. I've got some coloured crayons as well.'

Lucy's felt-tip pens had transformed into ordinary coloured crayons, but Mary's eyes filled with tears as she took them and examined them and then started to draw.

'Gosh Mary, that's awesome!'

'It's what?'

'I mean, it's good. It's really, really good! So let's start with the street. The houses are joined together, so it's a terraced street, isn't it? Shall I help you spell terrace? It's not written how it sounds.'

***

If James had felt peckish watching the ducks eat the stale bread that Ray had brought with him, he felt positively ravenous when he had to endure watching the couple eating fish and chips as they sat on a wall around the corner from the park. He was a little closer to them now and could hear their conversation. As there were other couples sitting on the wall, he figured there would be nothing too private about their conversation.

'Chips!' said Joan, 'Nothing like them when you are hungry, but when I've stuffed myself on them, the smell of them makes me feel proper queasy.'

'I know just what you mean,' replied Ray, 'My lodgings are just in the next street, and when I've had my tea at work and come home, I have to make sure the window in my room is shut because I can smell 'em from there.'

'You finished? I don't want to miss the last bus. Let's walk back.'

A few minutes later, they were at the bus stop, just a few yards from where Ray's motorcycle and sidecar was parked.

'Honestly, Joan, I don't mind giving you a lift. I'm a very careful rider, and I won't go fast.'

'No fear. You won't get me on that thing. It looks a proper boneshaker it does. Anyway, here's my bus. I've enjoyed my evening.'

'So have I. Can I see you again? I'm on the day shift all week.'

'Well, maybe Saturday, in the afternoon, I have to work in the mornings.'

'See you Saturday then. Let's meet in the cafe in the park in case it's raining.'

'Okay, bye.' With a shy wave, Joan leapt on the bus that had pulled to a halt. Ray waved back, pretended to play a trumpet, then returned to his motorbike, kick-started it into life and roared off in the opposite direction to the bus. James was all alone, none the wiser, but thankful for one piece of information that he had heard. Ray lived near the chip shop. So, hoping that Ray had gone straight home, James set off in that direction. He felt lucky, the first road he tried, 'Winchester Street', proved to be a good choice because there, parked in the street, next to number seven, was Ray's motorbike. James wished he knew what time Ray started work but resolved to be back before six the following morning to continue the surveillance. Right now, he needed to get back to the farm as quickly as possible. It would take him an hour, and he needed first of all to get away from the smell of chips and, secondly, get some sleep ready for the day ahead. Before that, though, maybe he would go home via the chip shop. He thought he saw a small tray of battered scraps on the counter that some people in the queue were snacking on as they waited. Maybe he could sample a few of those!

***

'You will be careful, won't you James,' lectured Robert, 'Don't go taking any stupid risks.'

'Of course, I will. I'm careful all the time now. I don't take anything for granted. I have to plan my every move.'

'After all, if anything happened to you, how would we

find you?'

'Don't worry; we haven't got any other choice. If we don't find Uncle Archie, we may never get away from the 1940s. We might end up dying of old age before we are even born!'

'Well, that's a bit of an exaggeration, but we would certainly be pretty old.'

'There aren't any elderly uncles and an aunt in the family photographs that might be us, are there?'

'Don't even think about it!'

***

At 7 o'clock, Ray descended the steps leading from 7 Winchester Road as though he were in a Hollywood musical. He was singing the trumpet part from 'One O'Clock Jump', a popular jazz tune made famous by Count Basie. He noticed the milkman opposite laughing at him, and so he gave him a theatrical bow, then kick-started his motorbike and set off for work.

Ten minutes later, Ray's good humour had waned. He halted his motorbike by the side of the road, climbed off it, and walked around to inspect the sidecar. He kicked the tyres; he frowned, peeled back the cover from the sidecar and peered inside. Then he kicked the tyres once again and climbed back on his motorbike. He couldn't afford to be late for work. What he was not to know was that, inside his sidecar, curled up at the bottom, lay James. His heart was pounding as he felt certain he was going to be discovered. For a moment, he felt another pang of fear as the bike stopped once again, but then he heard voices.

'You're cutting it a bit fine, sonny.'

'Yes, I know, sir. Had to stop because I think old Bertha here has a problem, riding funny she is. The weight's all wrong; feels like I've got a passenger, but I haven't, see.

I'll have to look at it later.'

'Dunno how you afford the petrol.'

'My earnings from the band just about cover it. Anyway, must get going. See ya!'

'Sir!'

'See ya, sir.'

After waiting for ten minutes, James had gained enough confidence to peel up the cover to the sidecar a little and peek through. In one direction, he could see a high wire fence, with barbed wire coiled across the top. To the other, he could see the brick wall of the single-storey building that Ray had parked next to. There was a military jeep and a row of army trucks, but little sign of life and no windows with a direct view of his position. James slithered out of the sidecar, carefully replaced the cover, and then stepped back to survey the scene.

The trucks were painted dark green; they were covered with a tarpaulin and had a bench seat running down each side of the interior. The backs were open, apart from the tailgate, and on each, there was hanging a sign roughly painted on a piece of wood. The first said 'Chestnut Anchester'; the second said 'Smith Melchurch'; the third said 'Price Anchester'. James had no time to work out the meaning of these signs because he heard a commotion, the sound of voices and footsteps and then, around the corner of the building, came a soldier, followed by a crowd of people approaching the very place where he was standing. Quickly, James sprinted back towards the perimeter fence, where he sensed he would be out of the way to watch what was happening. What he saw was puzzling to him. There were lots of people dressed in overalls, men as well as women, and of a wide range of ages. All were adult, but some looked quite old. They were chatting quite freely amongst themselves, but James was too far away to catch anything they were saying. They clearly seemed to have done this before because they all climbed aboard the parked trucks without being told where to go, then a soldier climbed into the back of each truck, another into the driver's seat, then slowly they set off for the entrance. The guard swung open the gates, then some of the trucks turned left down the road, the others turned right, and James found himself alone again.

This was not what James had expected. He knew he was coming to a prison, so he imagined it would be an imposing, solid building with large wooden doors and rows of windows with bars but, as he rounded the corner to the brick building, he saw before him rows and rows of wooden huts. First, he thought he would check out what the brick building was. He peered through a window, and inside he could see tables and chairs set out and, at the end of the room, a counter, behind which a man with a chef's hat on was wiping the surfaces. It was a staff canteen.

Next, James headed off in the direction of the wooden huts. They were long, painted black, with steps leading up to a door. Rather than risk opening the door, James climbed onto a metal dustbin that was positioned next to the first hut, and from here, he could see through one of the windows. Inside he saw rows of metal, single beds. Beside each bed, there was a small wooden locker. On these, he could see that some had a display of family photographs in an attempt to make the accommodation more homely. This must be where the people who climbed into the trucks lived! He thought it was unlikely that he would find Uncle Archie in one of these huts. He could see that beyond the huts were a number of two-storey brick buildings. They looked more promising, but before he set off in that direction, he heard a voice that he recognised. It was Ray, and he was speaking to someone.

'I tell you, I do this every day, I get him his breakfast, and he hardly eats a thing, eats like a sparrow he does.'

'He's probably used to that foreign food. What's it them Germans eat, Schnitzels or something?'

'And they eat sausages, don't they? Little chipolatas. Not like a decent English sausage.'

'Well, actually, they haven't been too decent lately – full of breadcrumbs they are. I reckon the cooks are taking all the pork home.'

This was a stroke of luck. James knew that Ray was guarding Uncle Archie so, instead of exploring the rest of the camp, James reverted back to his earlier role of trailing Ray. He followed him back to the canteen and waited outside. The sound of vehicles arriving prompted James to look around the corner of the building, and he saw that some of the trucks that he had watched leave the building earlier were now returning without their passengers. A few minutes later, Ray emerged carrying a metal box with a lid, and two handles on the side and, once again, James fell in behind him. When Ray arrived at one of the brick buildings at the far end of the camp, he put the box down on the ground and fished in his pocket for a key. He opened the door and, leaving the key in the door he moved the box to keep the door open, after which he stepped over it, retrieved the key and put it in the other side of the door. Then he slid the box out of the way with his foot, closed the door and locked it from the other side.

'A missed opportunity. Now how am I going to get in?' thought James. There was a way of gaining entry that he had used before, so it might work again. James walked over to the building. There was a window around the corner from the door. He knocked hard on it, then rushed back to the door and waited. Nothing happened. He returned to the side of the building and knocked hard on the next window, and again sprinted back to the door. Only partial success this time. He heard the sound of the window opening, a pause, then the sound of it shutting again. He repeated the exercise and achieved the same results. Once again, he knocked on the window, and this time a burly soldier appeared at the door and rushed round to the corner of the building to see who was causing the commotion. Before the door had slammed shut, James had thrust out a foot to stop it and quickly slipped through. Aware that an angry soldier might be returning, he made his way quickly down the corridor and stood out of the way in the corner to get his bearings.

After the soldier had stomped his way back into his office, James started to investigate the building. It was a fairly small dingy building with a central corridor and rooms to either side of it. The doors were all painted a uniform grey, and each had a small glass window through which James peered. He discovered that all the rooms on the ground floor were offices. Most of them were empty; in some, there were clerks bent over their paperwork. At the end of the corridor was a staircase leading to the next floor. The first room was a large office, and in it, James spied Ray who, with a mug of tea in hand, was talking animatedly to another soldier. The corridor in front of James looked identical to the one downstairs, save for the fact that, apart from the office where Ray was, all the wooden doors had been replaced with doors that reminded James of the railings in the park. These were prison doors. This was more like it!

CHAPTER ELEVEN

Robert was in his element. A cheer rang out as his bat swung, and the ball sliced through the fielders, earning his team another four runs. At last, he was in a position to prove his worth as a sportsman, for on the cricket field, everyone was under close scrutiny from the umpire, and unlike in the cross-country run, there was no opportunity for the opposing side to cheat. All his enemies opposed him because the boys had been divided into two teams; the local boys on one side and the evacuees on the other. There wasn't much integration at the school. Generally, the evacuees all stuck together, seeing the local boys as country bumpkins. However, perhaps from a combination of healthier and more plentiful food available in the country, and the hard physical work that many of the local boys had to undertake, generally, the evacuees were smaller and weaker than the local children. Cricket was not the favoured sport of the evacuees, whereas some of the local boys played in village teams. The evacuees all preferred football.

Robert's team had fielded first. The teacher had insisted that all the boys took a turn at bowling and, as a consequence, the local boys had racked up an impressive score. It was only when it was Robert's turn to bowl that the other team encountered any serious opposition, for it was then that in rapid succession, four boys were bowled out, and another one was caught. It was a match with a fixed number of overs, and now it was Robert's team's turn to bat. Robert had placed himself sixth in the order of batsmen, but it was not long before those before him were bowled out, and it was his turn to stand at the crease. Now that he knew that the others further down the batting order had little expertise at the sport, he devised a new strategy. Where possible, he would smash the ball to the boundary to ensure that not only did it score four runs, but it would also ensure that he stayed in position to face the next ball. If it were the end of the over, the sixth ball, he would play a defensive shot and take just a single run, so when the bowling changed ends at the end of the over, he would be in the right place to face the next ball.

Gradually, Robert brought up the evacuees' total to within range of the score they were chasing, and it was now the last over. Robert needed to score ten more runs to win. He was facing Kevin McGreggor. The first two balls had followed a familiar pattern and had crossed the boundary to score four points, but now Kevin McGreggor had devised a new tactic. This was quite apparent to Robert, as the third and fourth balls bounced up and forced him to duck as they whistled past his head. The aim now was not to try and hit the wickets, but to try and prevent Robert scoring and, as far as Kevin McGreggor was concerned, if the ball were to hit Robert in the process, then that would be even better! Robert noticed that the previous two balls had bounced short to roughly the same position and decided that, with only two more balls to go, he had to take a chance. As Kevin McGreggor released the ball, Robert took two rapid steps forwards, swung his bat and heard the satisfying thud as bat met ball. Another cheer rang out from the evacuees as they watched the ball sail through the air and cross the boundary without bouncing to score six runs. Victory was theirs, with one run to spare. Robert jumped up and shouting 'Yes!' he made a fist and punched the air, a gesture he felt afterwards probably owed more to his own time than to 1940s Britain, but it felt sweet to be the victor for once. Maybe now his luck had changed.

***

James, too felt his luck had changed as he slowly advanced down the corridor. All the rooms he passed were empty, but he was focused on one particular room halfway down the corridor because it was the only room where a chair had been positioned outside. When he was level with it, he saw that, on the chair, was the metal container that he had seen Ray carrying and, on the floor, resting where it had been pushed through the gap at the bottom of the door, was a plate of bread and butter and a congealed bowl of porridge. More importantly, lying on a narrow bed at the back of the cell was a figure wrapped in a blanket with his back to the door. Could this be Uncle Archie? First, James had to check the other cells. He silently sprinted down the corridor. All the rooms were empty, so he returned to the cell he had just left, moved closer to the railings, and, in a loud whisper, he tried to rouse the prisoner on the bed.

'Uncle Archie! Uncle Archie!'

The person lying on the bed suddenly sat up, alarmed because he had not told anybody his name, and there was also something familiar about that voice, something about it that seemed out of place in these surroundings.

'Uncle Archie!'

'What? Who are you? Where are you?'

'Uncle Archie, it's me, James.'

'James? James? James Baxter? Is this a trick? Where are you?'

'I'm right here in front of the door Uncle Archie; only you can't see me. No one can. I'm invisible.'

'My God! What are you doing here?'

'We came to look for you, Uncle. What is this place? Who are those other people who were taken away in trucks?'

'It's two things really; it's a military prison, and right now, I believe that I am the only guest. Only sometimes the occasional soldier who has drunk too much or got in a fight has the pleasure of a short stay here. It's also a kind of internment camp for refugees or people the Government doesn't trust; maybe they were born in Germany or Italy or married to people who are now our enemies. They are locked up here at night, but in the day, they have to work on the farms.'

'Gosh! I didn't realise that kind of thing happened here!'

'But you must tell me, how you came to be here, and what about Robert and Lucy?'

'Well, it's a long story Uncle Archie, but first of all, have you finished with that breakfast? I'm starving.'

Thirty minutes later, Ray nudged open the door to the office, holding the metal container containing the empty plate and bowl that he had just picked up from the cell.

'Well, I don't believe it, Sarge! This is the first time he has eaten all his food. He normally just picks at it, but these plates have been licked clean. Not only that, when I went down the corridor, I could hear him talking to himself. It was like he was asking himself questions and then answering in a different voice. He shut up as soon as he heard me coming, but I tell you, Sarge, I reckon he's going barmy.'

'You keep this quiet Private, I think he's a spy... you think he's a spy... and if he is a spy, we'll shoot him! We don't want no doctors poking their noses into it before the Ministry sends us this investigator. You're going to have to spend more time out there on guard.'

'Yes, sir. Fancy a brew first, though?'

Out in the corridor, James and Archie had resumed their conversation.

'So that's it, Uncle Archie. Here we all are stuck in 1940.'

'Oh, this is a much worse situation than I ever wanted to happen, but there is a way for you to get back, only it might take me a little time to work it out. There is a safety mechanism; I call it The Guinea Gap. I don't suppose you know what a guinea is?'

'I do, actually! I went to a maths lesson and helped Robert and Lucy, would you believe? One guinea is one pound and one shilling; two guineas are two pounds and two shillings and so on.'

'Very good! Well, my calculations involve taking each day that you were away and adding an extra hour. So if, for instance, you were supposed to go back at two o'clock on a

Saturday and you missed your slot, you could have gone at three o'clock on the Sunday, or, on the Monday, it would have been at four o'clock. Unfortunately, though, after each week goes by, there are some more tricky calculations. I don't suppose you can smuggle me a pencil and a piece of paper, can you? I might make mistakes if I try and do it in my head.'

'I'll have a little look around and be back as soon as I can.'

James found himself in a familiar position, following Private Raymond Taylor. Ray, carrying two mugs of tea, backed into the door of the office to open it. He didn't notice that it took a little longer to close than normal because James was holding it open as he slid past the reversing soldier. Nor did Ray notice that the door came to rest without slamming shut as it normally did. James released the door gently so that it didn't close properly; he wanted to make his route prepared for a quick and easy escape. From here, it was all fairly straightforward. Whilst the two soldiers chatted and drank their tea, James crept over to a waste paper bin because there he could see a piece of paper that had been screwed up into a ball. He squatted down and held it in his hands until it disappeared from sight. Then he turned his attention to looking for a pencil. He could only see one, and it was on the desk in front of the sergeant. The sergeant appeared to have been adding up rows of figures. James leaned across the desk and held onto the pencil, waiting for it to disappear and praying that the sergeant's attention would remain focused on his cup of tea. Just as the sergeant noisily drained his mug, James was able to retreat towards the door with the now invisible pencil.

'Another brew, sir?' asked Ray.

'You, my lad, are trying my patience. You're just trying

to put off doing your duty and sitting out there and guarding our prisoner. I want you out there, Private, for the rest of the day, and I want you to make a note of anything he says.'

'Yes sir, if you say so, sir. Can I borrow a pencil?'

'I do say so, Private. Now, where's that pencil I was using? Has it rolled on the floor?'

Whilst the two soldiers began their hunt for the pencil by peering under the desk, James silently opened the door and ran down the corridor back to Uncle Archie's cell.

'We haven't got much time. The guard, Ray, has been told he has to sit out here for the rest of the day. Hold your hand out, Uncle Archie. I'll put a pencil and paper in it. They will reappear in a few minutes.'

'Oh dear, it will take me quite a time to work out the calculations so that you can get back to your own time.'

'I'll come back tomorrow.'

'You really are a plucky young boy, but don't take any risks.'

'I won't. Save me some breakfast. Shh! He's coming now.'

James patted Uncle Archie on the shoulder, then tiptoed back up the corridor, flattening himself to the wall as Ray passed him; then, quickly, he descended the stairs and left the building. He figured that he had a couple of hours to kill, so he thought he may as well first visit the canteen to see if there were any leftovers to be had.

***

'Excuse me, sonny,' said a voice. Robert and Lucy had just left the school gates on their way home. For once, Mary was not with them; she had to stay behind in detention for failing a spelling test. Robert's heart was thumping. He hoped that their true identity had not been discovered.

'Yes, sir,' he answered politely to a man wearing a raincoat and a wide-brimmed hat. He feared the worst.

'I'm presuming that you are one of the evacuees as I have not seen you before today.'

'Yes sir'

'Well, you probably didn't notice me, but I was standing at the edge of the field watching you play cricket, and a very fine game you played.'

'Thank you.'

'My name is Richard Forbes, I am on the committee of the Anchester Town Cricket Club, and I was wondering if you would like to come for a trial.'

'Oh my!' gasped Robert, relief flooding into his voice. 'Well, I'm very honoured, sir, but I don't know how long we will be staying.'

'We may have to go back home,' chipped in Lucy.

'But if we are around longer, I would love to give it a go,' replied Robert. 'Are you in the team, sir?'

'Oh no, on account of this,' replied Richard Forbes, twisting around so that Robert and Lucy could see that one sleeve of his jacket was pinned up. He only had one arm.

'Oh gosh. I'm terribly sorry, sir. I didn't notice.'

'I used to play but lost my arm in combat during the last war.'

'Oh, that must have been awful!' said Lucy.

'It's not something I talk about.'

'Did you know our teacher, Mr Greville?' asked Robert. 'He's always talking about the war. I think he must have been some kind of hero.'

'Hero!' laughed Richard Forbes bitterly, 'no one that I know who fought in the war ever talks about it. It was supposed to be the war to end all wars.'

'Mr Greville talks about it all the time.'

'Well, let me say this, Greville certainly went to the trenches, and he will have seen some things, but as far as being a hero is concerned, I think he spent a lot of time recovering from the shock of it, and the mind plays funny tricks. However, there is a shortage of teachers at the moment, so I will say no more about it. Anyway, come down and see us, sonny, if you fancy a trial. Good day to you.' And with that, he turned and walked off in the opposite direction.

'Well!' said Robert, 'Just wait until I tell..'

'Don't you dare!' interrupted Lucy, 'I had decided that I didn't like Mr Greville, not one bit, but now I think differently.'

'How do you mean? He's every bit as much of a bully as the McGreggors are.'

'No, but it's not his fault that he is like that; now I feel sorry for him.'

'Well, I suppose you are right, but I won't be putting him on my Christmas card list!'

'Let's hope we're not still here at Christmas. I wonder how James is getting on. It's hard getting used to a world without mobile phones. Normally, even if he couldn't phone, he could send us a text. It's awful just having to wait.'

***

Back at the farm, Joe and the Land girls were working in the sugar beet field.

'I've never heard of sugar beet before,' said Joan.

'Me neither.'

'I've never grown it before', replied Joe, 'It's on account of them U-boats torpedoing our Merchant Navy ships. They can't get the sugar cane here no more so they have to make sugar out of this.'

'Can they make it into bananas? I could murder a banana right now!'

'Joe! Joe!' It was Martha, running across the field waving something.

'Joe, it's a letter. It's a letter from our Billy!' she shouted. Arriving at where Joe was standing, Martha had to pause for several minutes to get her breath back before she continued.

'He's back in England because he's been injured. He says he's alright; it's just a broken leg, he says, and when it's mended, he will have to go back, but right now, he's in a hospital because he has to lie down with his leg up in the air. He's down in Dover. I want to go and see him, Joe. I want to see our Billy.'

'Dover? How will we get to Dover, and what about the farm?'

'I want to go, Joe, he's our only son, so we're going. We can catch a train, and the girls can look after the farm, and them kids are old enough to look after themselves. We are going, and that's that!'

Well, we don't have to rush down there, do we? It's not like he's going anywhere. I can't miss market day. We will have to go next week. Monday maybe.'

***

James was feeling rather pleased with himself. He had found Uncle Archie, and he had also found rich pickings in the canteen. There was a large metal container full of left-over sausages that had been put to one side before they continued their journey to a large metal bin outside; a journey that would end in a trough to fatten a pig, a pig that would have to put up with the fact that there were five fewer sausages than there might have been had James not chanced upon them! Now James was laid full-length in the back of one of the trucks, catching up on lost sleep. He was awoken sometime later by the noise of the engine starting. The convoy of trucks once again pulled away and left the prison. James had purposefully chosen one of the trucks that had an Anchester sign hanging on the tailgate. He moved to the back of the truck and peered out. He needed to memorise the route in case he had to find the prison under his own steam, a task that was trickier than normal because all the road signs had been removed. Finally, the truck stopped at the side of the road outside a farm. He could see the waiting prisoners sitting under a tree at the side of the road, so he quickly climbed out of the truck, although the prisoners and their guards were in no particular hurry to climb in.

In the distance, James could hear the sound of a train.

'That might help me get my bearings,' he thought. He crossed the road to where there was a stile and where a footpath crossed the fields. He climbed on the fence to get a higher viewpoint, and then, recognising a tree two fields away, he knew exactly where he was. He was less than a mile away from Joe and Martha's farm!

When James arrived back at the farm, he found Robert and Lucy in the barn. They had been anxiously awaiting his return.

'Oh, thank heavens you're safe!' exclaimed Lucy, 'Tell us all about your day.'

'Well,' said James, 'The important news is that I have found Uncle Archie. He is in a military prison, and he is safe and well.'

'Brilliant!' said Robert.

'There's more. He knows of a way to get us back. It's called The Guinea Gap; only it's complicated. He has to work out calculations based on the day and hour we arrived, and he can work out when there are dates when we can travel home. Only he needed time to do it, so I'm going back tomorrow.'

'Fantastic!' said Robert.

'Was it dangerous, were you safe?' asked Lucy.

'I was careful. Let me tell you all about it. It started with a ride on a motorbike…'

***

James had no intention of travelling in a motorcycle sidecar again. The next morning he was perched on the stile opposite Chestnut farm, waiting for his lift back to the prison. Or, more correctly, he was waiting for the truck to arrive, bringing the prisoners to work on the farm, and he intended climbing in the back and hitching a lift back to the prison. All went to plan, the truck arrived, and the prisoners climbed out, some chatting loudly, others in morose silence, and they filed through the farm gates to start another day's work in the fields. Quickly, James climbed into the truck and, shortly after, it set off back to the prison. The driver was keen to get back to the prison to get another cup of tea, his third of the morning, and James was keen to get back and see Uncle Archie.

When James jumped out of the truck, he immediately sped to the building where Uncle Archie was being held. He hoped that what he had observed the previous day was part of a routine, for then the trucks had started to arrive back at the prison at the same time as Ray had been in the canteen collecting Uncle Archie's breakfast. Rather than resorting to banging on windows to trick his way in, James wanted to slip through the door either when Ray came out or when he returned with the breakfast. He heard the sound of Ray whistling as he walked back to the building, carrying the metal container. James remembered the actions from the day before and flattened himself against the wall by the side of the door. Again, Ray put the container down, fished for a key in his pocket and opened the door, then propped the door open with the container before stepping in and retrieving the key. Before he had a chance to shut the door, James leapt over the tin and, quickly and silently, ran down the corridor. Ray paused momentarily, feeling James' presence, then, looking around and seeing no one, he continued to lock the door.

James dashed up to Uncle Archie's cell.

'Uncle Archie. I am here, but your breakfast is on its way too, so I'll wait further down the corridor until Ray has gone.'

'Good boy! Glad to hear your voice. Shh!'

Down the corridor came the sound of Ray's boots. It was quite a distinctive sound because it bore no relation to the sound of marching soldiers; instead, there were taps and clicks and sliding sounds. Ray was practising his soft shoe shuffle! He placed the container on the chair, took out a metal bowl and a plate and pushed them through the gap at the bottom of the door.

'Enjoy your breakfast. It's the last one you are going to have.'

James clasped his hands over his mouth to stop any sound escaping as he gasped in horror, 'Did that mean they were going to shoot Uncle Archie?' Clearly, Archie had a similar thought, too, because it made Ray laugh.

'Ha ha! Got you! The look on your face, it's a proper picture. Nah, what I mean is it's your last breakfast here. We will soon be shut of you, and life can get back to normal. They're coming to take you away after lunch to a secret location. They're expecting you to have some answers for them, mind.'

Once Ray had returned to the office, James came back to the cell door. Archie pushed the bowl of porridge back through the door to James.

'Help yourself, my boy. I've lost my appetite since I've been in here anyway. Still, I needed to go on a diet.'

'It must be terrible for you cooped up in there.'

'Well, I am up a lot during the night, when no one can see me, and I try and keep fit by doing some exercises and then I spend a lot of time asleep during the day or pretending to be asleep whilst I work out what I might say when someone does come to ask me some questions. It looks like you found me just in time.'

'So they are going to take you off somewhere. Do you think I should come, otherwise we won't know where you are? Or should I try and steal some keys and get you out of here?'

'No, no, that's all too dangerous. Now quickly, take this paper in case he comes back. I've written down the information you need to get back - the 'Guinea Gap' dates for this month - you see, the longer you leave it the further apart the dates get. It's a factor of four; if you can't go this month it will be in four months, then if not then it will be sixteen months, you see, four times four, and then if not then, sixteen times sixteen is over twenty-one years away. So you have to concentrate on getting back as safely and as quickly as you can.'

'But what about you? How can we bring you back?'

'If you turn over the paper, you can see that I've written down the settings for the machine to locate and transport me. If it is operated from the machine itself, you don't have to go back to the same place in order to get transported back. The machine will find me wherever I am.

So you see, you really don't need to follow me. You just need to get home.'

'Will I still be invisible?'

'First things first, my boy, let's get you home. Now, would you like some bread?'

***

'I've got some news,' said Mary, as she walked alongside Lucy on their way home from school. 'I am going back to my Mum's, so no more detentions for me. She's going to come and collect me on Sunday.'

'Oh, that is good news,' replied Lucy, 'But won't it be dangerous, with the bombing?'

'No, that's just it; she's going to be moving too. She's met someone. He's in the Navy, the American Navy, and he's going to be my new dad, well, after the war, and then we're going to move to America, after the war that is, well, if we win the war!'

'Oh, we will, I know we will. It will be good for you. The land of opportunity, they call it.'

'Do they? I'm a bit worried about it. Isn't it just cowboys and Indians?'

'Oh no, there is more to it than that. It's going to be a very important country. More important than England.'

'Oh, you are crazy!'

'Honestly, it will be great. You will keep on drawing, won't you? I think you are so good.'

'It's the only thing I really like doing. Anyway, his name is Hank; honestly, that's his name, Hank! Hank says my Mum's got to move to the country, away from the bombing, and he's paid the rent on a cottage in a little village, so that's where I'll be living.'

'Is he nice?'

'I expect so; I've never met him. That's why I'm going

back now: because my Mum wants me to meet him before he sails off somewhere.'

***

'We've had some news,' said Martha as they sat at the table in the kitchen eating fish pie. As it was a Friday, Joe was not with them because it was market day, and Joe usually stopped off for a few drinks with the other farmers after the market.

'Someone else with news!' thought Lucy. She was anxious to talk to James and hear his news. She and Robert knew he was there. Apart from the tap on the hand that they had both received, there were two telltale signs. Firstly, his special friend Jet the sheepdog had followed him into the room and was presumably lying at his feet in front of the cooker. Lucy could tell by the way that Jet lifted his head now and then that he was occasionally being stroked. The second and more obvious sign of James' presence was that, as Martha's back was turned away from the cooker, large portions of fish pie were flying out of the casserole dish that was resting on the hotplate and disappearing into James's mouth. Every now and then, a small portion came Jet's way too.

Martha proceeded to explain to Robert and Lucy that she and Joe were going to be travelling down to see their son on the Sunday and not coming back until late on Monday night, so they would have to look after themselves, but not to worry about the farm because the Land Girls would be around during the day and she would leave some cooked ham for them to eat. She also told them that they must make sure all the curtains were drawn at night because it was important to keep to the rules about the blackout so they wouldn't attract any German bombers.

Neither Robert nor Lucy had been back to the station

since the night when their plans to return to their own time had been thwarted by the air raid.

'What happened to the stationmaster and his family?' asked Lucy.

'Oh, they are all fine, no one was hurt, but they had to pull down their house. They've moved in with her parents now, down the bottom end of town.'

Jet jumped up and barked and then ran to the door, his tail wagging. Moments later, they heard the sound of Joe arriving back. He usually travelled by horse and cart on market day, and it always proved useful after he had been to the pub because it didn't matter if he nodded off. The horse knew its way home. Martha returned to the oven and served Joe a portion of fish pie, frowning as she did so because she was surprised at how much they had all eaten.

'How was your son injured?' asked Robert, 'Was there a battle?'

'No, silly fool fell down the stairs,' replied Joe as he entered the room.' There must have been a storm; maybe the boat was rocking, we don't know. Navy, I ask you! Silly fool'

'Joe! You are drunk!'

'Well, that's as maybe, but I'll be sober in the morning, but that boy will still be a fool.'

'Joe!!!'

At last, the three Baxter children had the chance to escape the kitchen and were able to catch up with James' news. They had been sent out to the barn to collect, wash and sort the eggs. The kettle was boiling on the stove, and Lucy had topped up the bucket of water to warm it up a little. Joe had muttered to himself:

'Namby-pamby city folk.'

Clearly, Joe was in a very grumpy mood, and it would

be best to keep out of his way!

'Well, the good news,' said James, 'is that Uncle Archie has given us lots of information, and it's all written down on a piece of paper. I haven't looked at it yet. I thought we would do that all together. He says it has the dates we can go back, and the formula of how to work out the dates, and the settings on the machine to bring him back too.'

'And the bad news?' asked Robert.

'Well, there's two lots of bad news, well they're not necessarily bad. Firstly, if we don't go on the next date, we will have to wait another four months, and if we miss that we will have to wait over a year, and if we miss that, well it doesn't bear thinking about.'

'Oh no!' said Robert, 'What else?'

'Uncle Archie has been moved somewhere else, and I don't know where. I watched them put him in the back of a truck under armed guard, and then it drove away, but he said it won't matter. We can bring him back wherever he is if we are in control of the machine. I asked him what it was called, by the way, the Runic Block machine we called it, but he said he just calls it 'the machine.' Uncle Archie is planning to try and convince them that he has amnesia so that we have time to get home and bring him back.'

'Let's look at these dates then, James,' said Lucy, 'Set the paper out so we can see it.'

James spread out the paper on the barn floor, and they waited for it to appear. At the top of the paper, in the spidery handwriting that they recognised from Uncle Archie's notebooks, was written the date for the following Sunday at 9.30 pm.

'Sunday!' exclaimed Lucy, 'Everything is happening all at once. My friend Mary is going on Sunday, and Joe and Martha are going to see their son on Sunday, and now us.'

***

Saturday was a strange day. They spent it in a mood of nervous anticipation and wished for it to be over as soon as possible. James and Robert worked on the vegetable garden. Robert was proud of his efforts; there was barely a weed to be seen, and the tips of the lettuce he had sown were beginning to break the surface of the soil. Once Lucy had done her chores, she joined James and Robert at the vegetable patch.

'What should we do about our homework?' asked Lucy.'

'Well, I think we should have an optimistic attitude and presume that, by the time Monday is here, we will be back home in our own time, so there is no point doing it.'

'Trust you!' said Lucy. 'I'll tell you what I am going to do. I am going to write a letter to Joe and Martha. They don't know what my handwriting looks like, so I am going to pretend that it's from our mother and say that she has come to take us back home, like Mary's mum is doing. I know we have had to work hard here doing chores, but they work hard themselves. That's just the way it is, so we can't just disappear without an explanation.'

'We can ask them to tell the school too,' said Robert, 'I would be quite happy never to see old Gravy Greville again.'

CHAPTER TWELVE

Sunday came at last. Joan and Jane joined them for breakfast. They didn't normally work on a Sunday, but they had agreed to look after the farm whilst Martha and Joe were away. They were not staying the night but would leave around 5.00 pm, once all the animals were fed, and would be back early the next morning.

'So, who is taking us to the station?' asked Joe, 'I don't see why we should walk.'

'How do you mean?' asked Jane.

'Who can drive a horse and cart?'

'Not me,' said Joan, 'you won't catch me on that thing.'

'I went on a donkey once at Blackpool,' said Jane.

'I'll give it a go!' said Robert, 'but I've never done it before.'

'Oh dear lord!' exclaimed Joe, 'Right, Robert and Jane. You'll come. I'll show you what to do on the way down. There's nothing to it really; the horse knows its own way back to the farm.'

'Can I have a lift into town?' asked Lucy, 'I want to say goodbye to my friend Mary. She's going back home later today.'

So, for Robert, the morning was quite enjoyable. Jane was quite happy to hand over the reins to him on the way back from the station, and he enjoyed the leisurely ride back to the farm. One thing he noticed was just how different the roads were. Only one car passed them on the whole journey back. It slowed to the same pace as the horse, and the driver wound down the window to have a conversation with Robert.

'That's Joe Sinclair's rig ennit?'

'Yes, sir, it is.'

'So where's Joe then?'

'He's gone to Dover, to see his son.'

'What! Joe Sinclair, gone down South? He's never left this county before, hardly ever left the town. Dover eh! Well I never!'

Meanwhile, Lucy was sitting on Mary's bed. She had a surprise for Mary because the previous night in the barn, she had opened James' case, which was hidden in the corner. She had wanted to borrow a pencil to write down another copy of Uncle Archie's valuable information in case the original was ever lost and had quite forgotten that James had arrived with a notebook too. As he hadn't been going to school, he hadn't needed it, and so now she had it with her as a present to give to Mary. On the first page, she had written at the bottom, 'Don't stop drawing. Believe in yourself.'

'Oh Lucy, you are such a good friend. I won't stop. In fact, I'm going to start now! Sit over there, and I'm going to draw you. So you can stop pulling funny faces at me.'

***

The afternoon was spent helping Joan and Jane around the farm. The children also made sure they were packed and ready to leave early. At five o'clock, Joan and Jane left to return to Greystones, and for once, Robert, James and Lucy were all able to sit around the farmhouse table eating a meal of ham, cheese and bread. They ate quickly because they were keen to get started with the next stage of their journey. Uncle Archie's calculations indicated that they had a one-hour time slot, starting at 7.30 pm, for them to be seated in the waiting room at the station.

'My suggestion is that we set off now, so we don't have to hurry,' said Robert. 'I would much rather wait at the station than hang around here.'

So, after they had tidied up and left the letter for Joe and Martha, pretending that their parents had collected them, and after James said a tearful goodbye to Jet, they picked up their suitcases and left the farm. In fact, James had to give Jet the ham bone to keep the dog occupied in case he followed them. As they had plenty of time, they decided that, rather than walking directly through town, they would take a more circular route so they would be less likely to meet anyone that might apprehend them. It was the route that Robert was very familiar with from his cross-country runs.

It was a strange evening, it was still light but very cloudy, and a mist was rolling across the fields from the East.

'What's that noise?' asked Lucy.

In the distance, they could hear a deep, droning hum,

punctuated by the sharp noise of ack-ack guns being fired.

'Germans!' gasped Robert, 'German planes!'

'Oh no! I hope they don't bomb the station again. Surely not?'

The noise of aircraft got louder and louder. Then suddenly, they heard a slightly different noise, an engine whining and spluttering, and then in the distance, perhaps two or three fields away came an explosion that lit up the trees, adding smoke to the already increasing mist.

'It's crashed! Look!'

They followed the line of Robert's pointing finger, and there in the sky, spiralling down a little too fast, they saw a parachute. Almost as though drawn by a magnet, it headed towards the large oak tree that stood in the next field, the same oak tree that Robert would run past on his cross-country runs. They heard the cries of the pilot as he crashed through the branches before coming to rest suspended upside-down in the air, one leg trapped at a very unusual angle in the fork of one of the boughs.

'What should we do?' said Lucy, 'We don't know if he is one of theirs or one of ours. We have to go and see.'

They hid their cases in the hedge, climbed over the gate, and ran towards the oak tree.

'Hello, are you alright?' called Robert.

'Oh mein Gott!'

'He's German,' whispered Lucy. He said, 'Oh my God!'

'Come back to the roadside,' said Robert. 'We need to decide what we are going to do.'

'They backed to the hedge, keeping a watchful eye on their first sight of the enemy.' However, their enemy appeared to be stuck fast and in a lot of pain because he once again started to moan.

'We can't just leave him,' said Lucy, 'He's hurt. We've got lots of time. Can't we find someone to tell?'

'I can run back and find another farm,' said Robert. 'It'll be quicker if I do it.'

'I know the way to a farm,' said James, 'I know a shortcut. It's the farm where the prisoners were working, where the truck dropped me off. I could show you where the path starts and then come back to Lucy.'

'I don't think we ought to leave her on her own with a German.'

'Oh, I'll be OK,' replied Lucy, 'He's not going anywhere, is he? Just hurry, please.'

'If you are sure?'

'Yes, go!'

Robert and James set off at a slow jog, with James leading from behind. He didn't want to trip Robert up, so also he kept up a commentary as he ran so Robert would know he was still there.

'Around this bend we go, past the tree, and then past two more trees, not this path, it's another one. There, that's where it is! Oh, look, there are some people around this bend. I'll keep quiet, but I will be right behind you.'

There was indeed a group of people, but they were hardly authority figures. Many of them were known to Robert: the evacuees Fred, Pete, Harry and Mike, Spike Munro, Jack and Kevin McGreggor amongst them. All the people he would describe as the school bullies. There were a few older youths he did not know, one of whom James recognised. It was Billy Munro, whom he had seen drunk in the town, and who had reportedly injured himself so he wouldn't be conscripted. He was carrying a pitchfork, and he was the first to speak.

'I ain't seen you round these parts. I reckon you are a German.' Billy advanced towards Robert holding his pitchfork at a menacing angle, 'Come on, lads'

'He ain't no German; he's at our school. He's one of them evacuees.'

'What are you doing out?' asked Robert.

'We heard a plane come down, so we are going to get ourselves some souvenirs, and if we find any Germans, we are going to stick 'em,' said Billy, prodding his pitchfork into the ground. Robert noticed that all of the boys had some kind of improvised weapon.

'Anyway,' said Spike, 'What are you doing out?'

'Er same as you. I thought I heard a plane.'

'Well, either you are with us or against us,' growled Billy.

'Oh, oh, I am with you,' stammered Robert. The group then started to argue amongst themselves about which way to continue their search, so James took advantage of the confusion to whisper in his brother's ear.

'We can't let them do that. I've got a plan. I will lead them in a different direction. You get away when you can and go back to Lucy. Where can we meet up afterwards?'

'How about by the tunnel?'

'Yes, good idea. Now just watch what happens.'

***

Lucy edged slowly back towards the tree.

'Bist du OK?' She couldn't think of the German word for OK, but she hoped he would understand.

'Bitte Fraulein, mir helfen.'

Lucy understood that phrase; she enjoyed German lessons at school but never imagined that she would ever be in a position where understanding German would be so crucial. He wanted her help, but what could she do?

'I can't. Ich kann nicht.'

'Bitte, Bitte, Bitte. Oh, please!'

'Ich kann nicht.'

'Mein bein, mein bein, bitte.'

Lucy stared up at him. He sounded in so much pain. 'Mein bein', he was crying out 'My Leg'.

'Aufgeben.'

Lucy did not know that word.

'Ich verstehe nicht, I don't understand'.

'Surrender, I surrender,' he said. He clutched at the pocket of his leather flying jacket, and a number of items rained down. Lucy stared at them for a moment and then gathered them up and ran back to her case. She couldn't think of anything else to do other than to keep them safe.

'Mein bruder, my brother, he will come soon.'

***

'Achtung!' shouted James.

The group fell silent.

'Achtung!'

'It's a German! Let's get him. Where is he? '

'Sweinehund,' shouted James as he moved to another vantage point, further down the lane. The group dashed in that direction, and Robert was swept along with them, praying that James would stay well away from danger. James, however, was not worried about being caught for, after all, he did not have to stay concealed. He simply had to shout as though he were hiding behind a bush or tree but, in actual fact, was out in the open, so he could easily make his way over the road out of harm's way.

'Messerschmitt!'

No, for James, his main concern was whether he was going to run out of German words because he was not as diligent as Lucy in German lessons! However, he knew how to put on the accent and make it convincing, and he had a feeling that the rest of the group probably knew less than he did.

'Ich heisse Wolfgang.'

The boys dashed further down the road. For once, Robert was not leading the pack in a race, he was trying to work his way to the back, but unfortunately, due to his limp, Billy Munro was at the back and kept pushing him forwards.

'Come on yer coward,' he growled, mistaking Robert's

motives.

A phrase from an advertising campaign came to James.

'Vorssprung durch technik', he was beginning to enjoy himself now, but he was a bit perturbed that Robert hadn't managed to escape. He decided that he needed to take a different route. There were woods ahead. Maybe Robert could give them the slip there.

'Becks lager Carlsberg!' actually, he knew Carlsberg was a Danish beer, but he knew the others would not know that.

***

Lucy's heart was pounding, she knew he was in great danger, and she had to think fast. She could only hope that Robert would be quick. She had no idea where James was, but she hoped that he would be safe, that he wouldn't take too many risks. Right now, she couldn't afford to wait. She had to take action. She could not bear to hear the cries of the German airman any longer. She had gone back to her case because, although she had barely registered what the objects that the airman had emptied out were, one of them had made her shudder. It was a long knife in a brown leather sheath. Now, beneath the tree, she tucked the knife, still in its sheath, into the waistband of her skirt, and she started to climb. One of the advantages of growing up with two older brothers was that she had always wanted to join in with their games, and she had no fear of climbing trees. In fact, before their parents had gone missing, she remembered that they used to have a treehouse.

'Enough reminiscing,' she thought. She needed to concentrate. She climbed steadily and carefully, stopping when she was above the airman and looked down to work out what to do. The airman had stopped moaning now, he seemed to have passed out, but she could hear his gasps of breath. He was still alive. There appeared to be two problems; his boot was wedged in a fork in the branches and, above, his parachute was tangled up in the tree. The branches were far too thick to break but Lucy could see that the airman's high, leather boots were laced up the front. Lucy took the knife out of the sheath and, with one hand holding on to a firm branch, she reached down, slipped the knife between the shoelaces, and start to cut. When she had finished this, she climbed further down, wedging herself between a branch and the tree trunk so that she had the use of both arms. She pulled the boot open as much as she could, but still, his foot was stuck fast. She got out the knife again and started to hack at the leather, trying to open it out further. Luckily the knife was very sharp, but it was still a tough job. Eventually, she had cut away enough leather to reveal most of the airman's foot; she had hoped that his foot would then just slip out, but it was still held fast. She reached across and grasped the airman's ankle, thinking that it was just as well that he was unconscious because this was going to hurt him. She braced herself and pulled the foot upwards. The foot became free just at the same time as the airman let out a great roar of pain. Lucy shrank back against the trunk in fear as the airman, still held by his parachute, swung out in a gentle arc before stopping a few feet above the ground, gently spinning. The cries from the airman had now subsided to a low moan again.

Lucy then climbed higher in the tree to where the parachute was trapped. It was made of silk. She inserted the knife into the fabric, just above the seam where the cords were fastened to the parachute and started to cut. It was much easier to cut than the airman's boots and, as she sliced through the fabric, the airman gradually started to descend until, finally, he was left standing balanced on one foot before toppling over and landing on his back.

***

James racked his brain, 'German words? I know, sports!...Beckenbauer, Klinsmann, Becker!'

There was a roar of anger from the gang chasing him as they vainly rushed towards the tree that they thought he was hiding behind. James had noticed that Robert was still unable to get away so, now he was in the woods. James' strategy was to try and spread the group out as widely as possible, which meant he had to dash from one side of the wood to the other. He didn't have to worry too much about making a noise, though, because his pursuers were making a lot of noise themselves, crashing and blundering about in the woods.

'Kraftwerk, das autobahn!'

Looking back, he could see that Robert was apart from most of the others. Only Billy Munro was close by him. James sneaked back closer to them then, standing behind a bush, he whispered in a voice loud enough for Billy to hear but not so loud as to draw attention from the others:

'Achtung!' James picked up a stick, and before it turned invisible, and when he was sure that Billy would see it coming, he threw it towards Billy. Billy ducked out of the way and, forgetting about Robert, he raised his pitchfork and dashed towards the bush. Meanwhile, James had circled around to the back of Robert and silently pulled him back in the opposite direction.

'Well done!' whispered Robert, 'If I wasn't so worried about us leaving Lucy, I would have found it quite funny.'

'You go back to her now. I'll keep them busy here just a little while longer.'

'I will see you at the entrance to the tunnel. It's not far

from the tree where Lucy is.'

'OK, see you.' James ran off back towards the searching boys.

'Volkswagen, Audi, Mercedes Benz!'

Robert sprinted back to the tree and, to his horror, he could see that the parachute, still caught in the tree, was flapping in the breeze, but there was no sign of either Lucy or the German airman.

'Lucy!'

'Here, Robert, behind the tree.'

As Robert entered the field, he could see the airman sitting with his back to the tree trunk and Lucy, beside him, seated on her case.

'Did you get help, Robert? Is James with you?'

'No, we couldn't get help, but James'll be back shortly. It's a long story, but we have to go.'

'But what about Hans?'

'Whose hands?'

'No, Hans. His name is Hans. Do you think he will be safe here?'

'Well,' said Robert pensively, thinking of the braying pack of boys he had left in the wood, 'Maybe not. I've got an idea, though. He looks in a bad way. Do you think he can walk?'

'Not without help, he keeps losing consciousness, and I don't know if his leg is broken.'

'Well, let's try. I'll support him on one side, the side with the bad leg. I presume it's the one with the missing boot? You have the other side. First, we need to free him from the harness attached to these parachute strings.'

Once he had released Hans from the parachute harness, Robert hauled him up, grasping him by the belt with one hand and wrapping the airman's arm around his own shoulder with his other hand. Lucy, holding onto her case with one hand, tucked herself under Hans' arm on his other side and, very slowly, they started across the field. Hans was both conscious and silent now as he focussed on trying to help their progress. It was not far to the tunnel where Robert had arranged to meet James, but they were travelling so slowly and awkwardly that it seemed miles away. It was made worse by the fact that, after a while, Hans once more started to slip into unconsciousness, meaning that they then had to support his full weight. Lucy was struggling because she was shorter than Robert and also because she refused to let go of her case. Just as she felt she had to rest, she heard a voice behind them.

'I'm back!' It was James; he had caught up. He took one look at the situation and then slipped in between Lucy and Hans and took the weight on his own shoulders. He figured that he had nothing to lose. No one else was around, and the German, with his head lolling down and his feet dragging behind, hardly looked a threat. Now they made much quicker progress. Every now and then, Hans raised his head and looked at Robert and Lucy before passing out again.

At last, they reached the tunnel.

'Put him down a moment and just wait here,' said Robert, 'I just have to check something.' Robert listened to check no trains were approaching, then ran down the tunnel. James and Lucy started up when they heard a crash; the sound of splintering wood, but then heard Robert's feet crunching on the gravel as he ran back.

'Come on. It's the little room that I ran past once on a cross-country run for a dare, 'Old Growler's room. I've just broken the door in. We can put him there.'

A few moments later, Hans was stretched out on the

wooden bench that ran the length of the storeroom. He was still wearing his leather airman's helmet, so Robert unfastened the strap below Hans' chin and pulled it off. He groaned, opened his eyes for a moment, then passed out again.

'Now what?' asked Robert. 'Have you any idea what time it is? It's awful not having a watch or a phone!'

'Well, we left the farm at 5.30, and that must have been about an hour ago, perhaps more. We have a one-hour slot starting from 7.30 to be in the waiting room, so I reckon we are still in time,' replied Lucy. 'I still don't like leaving him, though. He looks in a bad way. Who knows, he may have hit his head in the tree. He may have concussion. Someone ought to keep an eye on him.'

'I reckon if I run to the station from here, following the train tracks, I could get some help and then get back here in plenty of time. James could stay and keep guard. Give me half an hour. If I am not back by then, you should just set off for the station and get yourselves back to our own time. Have you got Uncle Archie's instructions? If you can bring him back, then he can work out how to bring me back.'

'Yes, I've got them; they are in my case,' said Lucy, patting the case beside her. 'Yes, go then, go quickly, but please be careful.'

'OK, but you be careful too. Remember, he is the enemy.'

As Robert turned to run out of the door, he noticed that Hans was coming back to life. He set off down the tunnel and realised that he was still holding onto the airman's helmet. He could have thrown it aside and collected it later, but he decided to hang on to it for the moment. Robert was not correctly dressed for optimum speed, and he had experienced a tiring hour or so; carrying the airman had been heavy work. He gritted his teeth and maintained a pace that was faster than normal. The adrenalin coursing through his veins made him forget his exhaustion and, before long, he was mounting the platform at the station.

'Oy! C'mere. Wot you doing down there? You're in trouble me lad!'

Robert was hauled up to his feet and felt strong hands grip him at the scruff of his neck.'

'Please, I need to speak to...'

'I'll tell you who you are going to speak to, my son. You are going to speak to the stationmaster and my sergeant; that's who you are going to speak to, and then you will have to answer to your parents because they are going to get a right earful.'

Robert kept quiet. The people he was being hauled in front of were just the ones he wanted to see.

'Sergeant, sir. I just caught this ruffian lurking about on the train tracks. He could be a spy or anything, sir.'

The soldier in the stationmaster's office sighed and stood up, as did the station master, an elderly gentleman with white hair and a bushy moustache.

'Well?' said the sergeant. 'Have you anything to say before I Cry 'Havoc!', and let slip the dogs of war?' He turned and spoke to the stationmaster, who rolled his eyes up to the ceiling.

'I'm wasted in this army, you know! What a piece of work is a man! How noble in reason!......'

This was not the greeting that Robert had expected, especially considering how rough the soldier who had brought him to the office was. Robert recognised these words; it was a quote he had heard on his first day in Mr

Greville's class, a play that James had acted in.'

'That's Shakespeare, isn't it, sir?'

'Well, well, not quite the ruffian you first appear to be.'

'Please, sir, I've come to get help. I came along the railway line because it was the quickest way.'

'He that is thy friend indeed. He will help thee in thy need.'

'Help with what?' snapped the stationmaster, growing weary of the sergeant's Shakespearean quotes.

'It's a German sir, he parachuted out of a plane only he was injured, so now my sister is looking after him. He's in the tunnel sir, there's a little room in the tunnel, and we put him in there. This is his helmet.'

'By God, there is a storeroom built into the side of the tunnel!' replied the stationmaster.

'A call to arms!' cried out the sergeant. He opened the door and yelled, 'Corporal, I want five men here now.' He then turned to the stationmaster.

'Which direction is the tunnel, and have you got one of those handcars, you know the ones with the handle that you pump, like in the silent films?'

'Well, actually we have, it's used for maintenance. There isn't another train due for an hour, so you can get your men to lift it onto the tracks. The tunnel is to the South.'

'I can show you, sir, my sister's there. I have to go back.'

Within five minutes, Robert, together with five soldiers and the Sergeant, were travelling back down the railway tracks. Two of the soldiers stood facing each other, each holding onto a large handle that they pumped up and down, causing the handcar to propel itself forward at speed back towards the tunnel. Despite his concern for James and

Lucy's safety, Robert, seated at the front of the little truck, allowed himself a few moments to enjoy the ride. When they entered the tunnel, Robert pointed to the doorway of the little storeroom, and the soldiers applied the brake, pulling on a large lever. Then they jumped down, shouldered their rifles and slowly advanced towards the door.

'Be careful!' exclaimed Robert, 'My sister's in there. I don't think you will need those guns. He has surrendered.'

The soldiers continued to creep towards the door. Robert noticed that the door opened, seemingly by itself. He guessed that what was actually happening was that James, who had been left on guard, had slipped into the room to alert Lucy to their impending arrival. Nevertheless, when three of the soldiers burst into the room, still pointing their rifles, it was still a shock for Lucy, who screamed in surprise. There was no need for such a dramatic entry because Hans was unconscious.

'We think he has broken his leg,' cried out Lucy. 'His name is Hans Schmidt.'

'Jones, Evans,' called out the sergeant, 'Lift him onto the handcar. We will take him back to the station. He's a prisoner-of-war now. There won't be room for you two kids on it, though. Can you make your way back to the station on foot?'

'No problem,' replied Robert, 'Come on Lucy, let's go.'

Robert felt a squeeze on his arm that reassured him that James was with them and hadn't got trampled when the soldiers burst into the room. Lucy grabbed her case from behind the door; both Robert and James realised at that moment that their cases were still hidden under a hedge, but they were not too bothered. Hopefully, they wouldn't need them again, and, with the knowledge that there was not another train due for some time, they walked along the train tracks at quite a brisk pace, only stepping aside as the handcar passed them.

When they eventually arrived back at the station, Lucy looked up at the clock.

'Gosh, it's later than I thought. We've only got five minutes!'

'Oy, you two!' called out the corporal. 'We want to talk to you.'

Robert and Lucy looked at each other anxiously. They had little time to spare. James squeezed Robert's arm as he started to think about diversionary tactics that might help them get away.

'Wait in the waiting room; we will be with you when the military police arrive to take away the prisoner.'

Relief flooded over Robert and Lucy's faces. The waiting room was just where they needed to be. They rushed over to the room but then found to their consternation, that the room was not empty. There was a family waiting for a train. It looked like a mother and two grandparents and, sitting on the window seat were two young children. James realised that this was a time for desperate measures – he crept over to the two children, a boy about seven and his sister who was a year or so older and, trying not to cause much pain, he pinched the girl on her cheek.

'Hey, stoppit!' called out the girl who pushed her brother, causing him to cry out and push her back.

'Will you two pack it in,' shouted the mother crossly, 'I've told you before, now come here the two of you. You can't be trusted to sit quietly, can you?'

The two children returned ruefully to their mother's side and, with a guilty smile, Lucy and Robert took their places on the window seat. James wasn't finished yet, though. He heard a commotion further down the platform, no doubt the military police had arrived, so he slipped back out of the open door and called out:

'Quick, look what's happening here!'

This had the desired effect. Without wondering where the voice was actually coming from, the family got to their feet and rushed to the door. James then stepped back into the room, pushed the door closed, ran over to the window seat and took his place between Robert and Lucy.

'Genius!' said Robert in approval. The three children held hands, and, almost immediately, they felt that fairground sensation that they were swooping down and up from blackness into light. They were on their way back to the 21st century!

CHAPTER THIRTEEN

'Oh at last!' cried out Lucy.

'Let's get out of this cubicle,' said Robert, 'Just in case the machine sends us off somewhere else.'

'What time is it? In fact, what day is it? I feel we have been away a whole lifetime.'

Robert looked down at his wrist. The whole time he had been away, he couldn't help doing this whenever he wanted to know the time, only to find that his wrist was bare. However, now he was pleased to see that his digital sports watch was back in its rightful place.

'I don't believe it! It's just after eight o'clock on the same day we set off. We've only been away for an hour!'

'Well, first things first,' replied Lucy, 'We've got to

reset the machine with the settings that Uncle Archie gave us, so we can bring him back. They are here in the pocket of my cardigan, and look!... You can still read them. I was worried that they wouldn't transport through time, but they have.'

For the next five minutes, they reacquainted themselves with the machine that had taken them back to the 1940s. They inserted the wooden blocks inscribed with the strange signs, turned switches and double-checked all the settings according to the instructions on the precious piece of paper. Then finally, when they were satisfied, all three of them stood around the machine and pressed the button labelled 'START'.

They had never been in the room when the machine was working before (apart from the times when they had been quickly whisked off into another time), and the experience was quite alarming. Bells rang, the computer gave a high-pitched whine and then started beeping, and the lights in the room began to flash. Then, behind the glass screen, there was a light so bright that they had to look away. The light faded, and when they looked back, there was Uncle Archie, sitting on the bench and grinning from ear to ear.

'Uncle Archie!'

'I can't tell you how happy I am to be back. Things were getting decidedly sticky back there.'

Archie emerged from behind the glass screen and surveyed all before him. Then all of a sudden, his smile faded.

'James, where are you, my boy?'

'I'm here, Uncle Archie'

James Robert and Lucy then realised why Uncle Archie's good mood had evaporated. It was James's condition that had led them all to travel back into time, and nothing had changed.

'So, did all go smoothly with your return? Did the machine behave itself?' asked Archie.

'Oh, the machine behaved itself alright,' said Robert, 'Only we had a very eventful day and got held up rescuing a German soldier from a gang out to stick pitchforks in him!'

'Oh dear,' exclaimed Lucy, clasping her hand to her mouth, 'I forgot to give him back the things that fell from his pocket.'

'What things?' asked James.

'I'm not sure, it was when I was left alone, and he was stuck up the tree. I put them in my bag. There was the knife that I used to cut him free from the parachute, but there were some other things. I wonder if they travelled through time?'

Lucy picked up her bag and reached inside. The first thing she pulled out was the last thing used: the knife. She placed it on the desk. She delved inside again and pulled out a small, flat rectangular object. No bigger than her hand, it was a kind of wallet, made of black leather and fastened with a metal clasp. She undid the clasp and opened it, revealing two black and white photographs. The first showed a family group standing outside a large house; she recognised Hans looking proud in his uniform, alongside two people whom she presumed were his mother and a younger sister. The other photograph was of a girl who looked a similar age to Hans; perhaps she was a girlfriend.

'Oh, I wish I could have given these back to him,' said Lucy.

Archie took them from her and had a closer look. He slipped the two photos out of the wallet and looked at the backs. They both had writing on them; the family group had an address written in small precise letters, an address in Austria. The photograph of the young woman had the words 'Ich liebe dich, Liesa,' with a large kiss written with a flourish.

'Well, maybe you can still return it to him,' said Uncle Archie. 'He may well still be alive. At least you know that, as he was taken prisoner, he is likely to have survived the war, and. as for his home, well, it looks to be very rural from the photograph, so maybe the house also survived. There was some terrible bombing on the industrial cities, so you could be in luck.'

'Oh good,' said Lucy, 'But there was something else, something heavy.' Again she delved into her bag and pulled out another leather object, and laid it on the desk next to the knife. Lucy gazed at it. She wasn't absolutely sure what it was, but she somehow felt reluctant to open this leather case to find out what was inside. Robert started forward to pick it up, but Archie, who realised instantly what it was, restrained his arm.

'No, let me, it's a pistol, and it's probably loaded.'

He carefully undid the clasp on the side of the leather holster and drew out a black pistol.

'Well, I never! It's a Walther PPK!'

'Where have I heard that name before?' asked Lucy.

Robert pointed to the blackboard. It was one of the names written up there.

'This is the very thing that I was looking for back in 1940,' exclaimed Archie. 'I had no idea how I would find it. I didn't think for a moment that it would find me!

'But why do you need it?' asked Lucy 'I don't understand.'

'And how is it connected to me?' asked James.

'Yes, you deserve an explanation,' replied Archie, 'It's

all quite complicated, but I will try. First of all, the machine isn't just what you see in front of you; in fact, the whole of the museum is part of the machine. It's all connected. There is a catalogue of exhibits on the machine's computer, and occasionally it throws up a glitch. A problem where something is missing. In this case, it is the pistol. Once I have scanned it, there is a drawer in the museum where it will be stored, and the balance will be restored.'

'But how does that affect me?'

'I was coming to that; it's all rather delicate. You know how you work as a team? Well, it was the same with me and your parents. I presume you know they were explorers and went missing when you were quite young? Well, they were not just exploring the world for the sake of it; they were hunting for missing artefacts for this museum. And, what's more, their DNA, as well as my own, is embedded into the programme that runs this machine. So you see, we are all connected in more ways than one.'

There was a pause as the children took in the enormity of the situation, broken when Archie sprang to his feet.

Well, we must take action, there's no time like the present. James, you must go back behind the screen and sit and wait.'

'Oh no!'

'I promise you that you won't go back in time. Go quickly. I will reset the machine.'

It took Archie around fifteen minutes to get the machine ready as he typed commands into the keyboard, inserted wooden blocks into slots and placed the pistol under the scanner.

'Ready!' he shouted. Robert and Lucy rushed over to the glass to watch. Archie pressed the 'START' button, the machine whirred into life, lights flashed, and a bell rang.

The room lights dimmed briefly, then returned to normal, and Archie, Robert and Lucy looked expectantly through the glass. Nothing had changed.

'Oh dear, dear me,' sighed Archie.'

'Oh James,' cried Lucy, and in a flash, she opened the glass door and rushed in to comfort him.

'Wait!' cried Archie, 'I haven't turned off the Machine yet.' It was too late. Lucy was already in and sitting next to James, giving him a hug.

'Lucy,' gasped Robert. He couldn't believe what he was seeing because he could see before him the shimmering outline of his brother James being held tightly by Lucy. He, too, rushed into the room.

'Of course! What an idiot I am,' cried out Archie, 'You are all linked. You all need to be there to make it work. Lucy, Robert, sit on either side of James and hold hands. I will start the machine from the beginning.'

Once again, the room lights dimmed, and bells rang, but this time, sitting between Robert and Lucy, with a beaming smile, sat a very visible James.

'Goodness!' exclaimed Lucy as she let go of his hand. 'You're filthy.'

'Well, washing was never that important when I was invisible.'

***

A week later, the Baxter children were all back at school. Actually, Lucy was at the Arts Centre in Anchester, together with her classmates, to visit the exhibition by the artist Mary Cairns. Lucy was pleased because, although she had briefly seen the exhibition before, it had been at a stressful time, as it was their first attempt at time travel. She and James had been so worried that Robert would not get there in time for the return journey because he had to run from the school. It was the last week of the exhibition, and now she had time to enjoy looking at the artwork.

She decided to start in order, with the earliest drawings first, and what she saw made her gasp with amazement. She had only fleetingly looked at this work before, but this time she was transfixed by a drawing of a farm that she had seen on her last visit to the gallery. She had given it little attention at that time. Then it was just a picture of a farm, but now she could see that it wasn't just any old farm, it was a farm that she knew very, very well. It was Highfield farm… Joe & Martha's farm. Not only that, she was present when it was drawn for, although the picture was dated 1940, for her it was just a few weeks ago when, one sunny afternoon, after school, her friend Mary had walked back to the farm with her. They had sat on the grassy bank outside the farm, and Mary had taken out the sketchbook that Lucy had given her and drawn this very picture. Lucy looked at the other pictures in the room. There was the picture of the Anchester street that she remembered, and next to it was the picture that Mary had drawn of Lucy whilst she sat on the bed in her bedroom. She remembered that Mary's mother had met an American sailor, so after the war, they must have all gone to America, and later Mary Ball must have married and become Mary Cairns!

***

Robert could hardly speak. He lay on his back, gasping for breath as he looked up at his school athletics sports coach.

'Well done, Robert. What a race! You were just flying. no one could touch you.'

Robert just nodded and raised a hand to acknowledge the compliment.

'This is the first time a boy from this school has come first because, as you know, it's open to all the local running clubs too. It's got a lot of history about it, this race, *The Anchester All-comers Cross Country*. They have been running this race for a hundred years. Not even the last war put a stop to it.'

Robert nodded. He was in total agreement because the route was identical to the race that he had run when he was at the local school back in 1940. It was the race that he would have won then if he hadn't been pounced upon by the gang of bullies.

'I've never seen you run so fast, and considering you have just come back after the Easter holiday...you must have put some training in!'

Robert pulled himself up to a seated position and, still too exhausted to talk, gave a noncommittal shrug. He thought to himself that, although everyone else had only been away from school for a short Easter holiday, he had been back in the 1940s for much longer and had played a lot of sport, plus he had found himself having to run to the station on a couple of occasions so he had kept up his fitness levels - but in a way that he couldn't possibly explain to the sports coach!

'Good show! Well, you will be receiving a medal from the Chairman of the Anchester Athletics Club. He used to be quite a runner back in the day himself, you know, in his eighties now. Spike Munro, they call him. Colourful character, little wiry chap. Heard him speak at a charity dinner once. Apparently, he fell in with a bad lot after the war, even went to prison, but he turned his life around through running. Do you good to meet him!'

'I've already met him,' thought Robert to himself, 'But I'm glad it's turned out well for him, so it would be good to meet him again.'

***

'Just listen to this review,' announced James to the other boys in the dormitory.

'James Baxter's interpretation of Under Milk Wood is quite simply a triumph. To take Dylan Thomas' play for radio, a play that one associates with all things Welsh, but to present it using the accent of our local Anchester is sheer genius. James Baxter has an uncanny ear: the range of voices that he created gives you the impression that he must have been a fly on the wall of the local shop, so natural were the conversations that he so smoothly delivered. Not only was the accent so good, and he is, after all, not a local boy, but there was something about the performance that reminded one of times gone by. So fitting for a play that began its life in the 1940s. This boy has a future!'

'That's a really good review, James. Who wrote that!'

'Hmm. Let me see. Ah yes, it was written by James Baxter.'

James wasn't in a position to say any more because he was buried under an avalanche of pillows thrown at him from every corner of the room.

EPILOGUE

Dear Miss Baxter,

I am writing to thank you so much for passing on to us the two photographs that you recently discovered. One of them is a picture of my mother and the other is of my father, my aunt and my grandmother.

I never knew my aunt or my grandmother as they both died during the war. Such terrible times! Unfortunately, my father has also passed away just a few weeks ago. He had been quite ill for some time, but I did get a chance to show him the photographs just before he died, and he got a great deal of pleasure from looking at them. He talked frequently about his 'English Angel' who saved him when he had to parachute from his aeroplane and got stuck in a tree. I suppose that was your grandmother.

The photographs now have pride of place on the shelf in my mother's house. She wanted to thank you herself, but she does not speak English so, on behalf of our whole family, we want to say thank you, not just for sending the photographs, but to your relatives, whether alive or not, for helping to return my father Hans Schmidt safely to us.

Forever in your debt,

Helga Schmidt

ACKNOWLEDGEMENTS

I wish to thank family and friends for their support. I would like to thank Elizabeth Newsham for creating illustrations for the book and Jessica Bell for the cover art. I especially want to thank Rachel Laurence, the actress who brought this story to life for the audio version. I also want to thank Chris de Verteuil, who wrote and performed original music for the audio recording.

I also owe a big thank you to my mother Joan Johnson - she was a Land Army girl from Birmingham, and during the war, she found herself on a farm washing eggs in cold water!

Joan Johnson, on the left with Joyce, the cow-man's daughter 1945.

A NOTE FROM THE AUTHOR

 I hope you have enjoyed this book. The story continues!
Please look out for the next book in this series: an adventure where Lucy, Robert and James find themselves stuck once more - Stuck 1595: An Elizabethan Adventure

'…. James had endured the worst three days of his life. He was shivering, not just because he had spent long hours hidden from view under sacking in the back of an open cart, but also from fear. He remembered Uncle Archie's warnings about the violent times they would be arriving in, and he was haunted by the brief flash of the knife that

Scarface had waved in front of him. He was hungry too, he had not been fed since he was seized, and he was bruised, not so much from the rough treatment by his captors, but more from the fact that the many ruts and holes in the road had caused him to be thrown around in the back of the cart. A new sound told him that they were entering a town or city; the metal wheels of the cart now clattered along paved roads. Finally, the cart stopped. James awaited his future with trepidation.'

Would you like to read more books in this series?

 You can order the 'Stuck' series from Amazon by visiting this page on my website (they are all stand-alone books): www.stuckdave.co.uk/blink

You can also join my mailing list and find information about upcoming publications and have the opportunity to win free stuff! I would love it if you followed me on Instagram, too: @stuckdavewrites

Finally, I would really appreciate it if you could write a review on Amazon of my book. Even if you did not buy this book yourself from Amazon, you should still be able to post a review there.

Printed in Great Britain
by Amazon

18086939R00123